A glimpse of
light found

Glimm

A glimpse of light found

Glimm

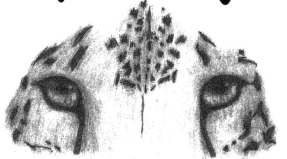

B. A. Hughes

Illustrated by Quinci Woodall

I proudly dedicate my first published work
to my 13 grandchildren for whom I write.

Love,
Mimi

Glimm
Light Flown

Glimm galled, where went the day?
Shattered, scattered, flown away
Sparkle died in logic's tide
Digits disemboweled his life.

Glimm called, that's all there is?
Numbers, lines, bytes and bits?
Look again, Glimm, beat his heart
Starflash, Earthlore, song and art.

Glimm saw the sun arise
Gave his heart to ancient eyes
Bowed his knee, sang aloud
Glimpse of glimmer, gift of God.

—B. A. Hughes

Published by Four Cats Publishing LLC

Cover design and cover photograph by Tonya Foreman
Cheetah cover image and interior illustrations by Quinci M. Woodall
Back cover author photo by Kelli Holdeman

Printed in the United States of America

ISBN-13: 978-0988839984
ISBN-10: 0988839989

To order additional copies, contact Four Cats Publishing LLC,
www.fourcatspublishing.com

Contents

Introduction

The stories presented in *Glimm, A Glimpse of Light Found* by B. A. Hughes touch on everyday mysteries and wonder. They may especially appeal to young people in the years before high school when natural curiosity may begin to wane. Suddenly, gadgetry, TV, sports, status, and appearances claim considerably more interest than requisite. Although formal or home schooling is a priority in our children's lives, wise mentors will also guide students toward exploring the natural and spiritual. At a young age, we all sense what is valuable or needed for our own good. However, developing and claiming our sense of self require many years, many life coaches, and much experience. Since a full lifetime is hardly enough time to discover all we are and can be, we must urge our students to seek out enlightenment from a variety of sources: loved ones, teachers, peers, sacred texts, and especially nature.

Since times before recorded history, **stories** have provided a guiding light. (For example, "Over that mountain and a little to the left, your Uncle Thud and Aunt Uga found a cave full of bears…guess what happened.") Indeed, stories like these have existential value! In fact, all wise stories and parables have such value to some extent. Good stories provide LIGHT to children of all ages: light as needed for daytime work; light as in edification; the magical light of discovery; illumination required to avoid danger and sense beauty; and the lighter side of life.

The underlying theme of the stories in this book is light—of truth, wonder, and self-discovery. Inspired by a deep respect for nature and family, a loving grandmother tells these tales from a kid's perspective. Into tedious school days and everyday annoyances from family and friends, mystical connections and animals appear that change our attitude toward life and its meaning. Into troublesome events, curiosity is reawakened. Even nature herself or a gadget transforms to deliver a new lesson. We don't have to be tweens or teens to appreciate the lessons in these enchanting stories.

Accompanying the stories are remarkable hand drawings by the young illustrator Quinci Woodall that highlight the majesty of the natural world. In addition, for classroom and homeschool studies, this book includes glossary terms[†] and story questions following each story, as well as story summaries and lessons in a Guide to Parents and Educators.

—Four Cats Publishing Editors

[†]Glossary terms in the text are highlighted with a dagger symbol.

Spots in the Wind

THE FABLE OF CHEETAH PRINT

for Annabelle

The giant sun glared. It shot through a squat leaning tree throwing only a bit of shade over Siel.[†] She leaned into the shade like a snake retreating under a rock. Her long flat tail swatted the short grasses into submission[†] like a jump rope slapping your playground gravel. A wind twisted the red and golden grass heads on their toothpick stems, and their shadows scurried across Siel's face. But Siel didn't scurry. She barely blinked her great kaleidoscope eyes.

She lifted her smart brown-black nose to catch a strange

dark scent. She rotated her head and her ears independently. She saw nothing but heard a faint **PLINK-SLAP**. It was a sound darting from the stream over the savannah[†] to her bed under the acacia tree.[†] A growl rolled deep in her throat, and the vibration rattled the flimsy, ferny leaves, dropping a few onto her back. She was vigilant, but nothing came of the scent or the sound.

So she stood and shook like springtime laundry on the clothesline. Siel gazed in every direction to oversee her homeland. The sun caught glints of every color in her eyes and shot its brightness all over her face. She loved the gentle slope of the grassy yellow plains, the few but demanding boulders, the scrub shrubs running in lengths like Texas fences, and the occasional merciful tree. Then she spied her neighbors, those odd beasts—not one as fast, sleek, or beautiful as she.

Now, the wind shifted and all she heard was the rustling of the Serengeti,[†] like wadding up a brown paper bag. Siel turned a complete circle, then two, just like a cat, and plopped down, hindquarters first, puffing dry dust two feet high. Siel relaxed with a deep sigh. Her taut ears drooped back s-l-o-w-l-y and her tail lay limp. She stretched out looking like a quilt tossed off your bed. Her rough pink tongue like a kitchen sponge groomed every inch of her Joseph's Coat of Many Colors[†]: black spots on a background of light browns, yellows, tans, and an occasional streak of orange. She preened[†] until sunspots of gold shone from her fur.

I am the most gorgeous of all the animals in the grasslands! Siel imagined those poor plain brown lions, those boring black and white and black and white and black and white zebras! *Even the silly yellow-splattered giraffes cannot compete with my cheetah design!* Siel snarled at the thought. The young cheetah had not learned the good manners of appreciating others who shared her part of the world. She bragged so much, in fact, that the other wild beasts steered clear of her.

Thirsty, Siel arose to swagger[†] toward the brilliant pool where the African sun is captured and ZINGS off in every direction. It is a giving stream. Siel looked cautiously over the dancing ripples, toward the underbrush edging the pool. Bits of pure sparkle humbled the drinking animals with momentary blindness. Siel was always stunned by the beauty of the clear water. *This is my cup, my mirror, my vanity*, she pondered. She gazed long at her reflection in the giving stream. But numerous of her neighbors were startled, braying[†] and skittering away from the waterhole. *Ah! They are just jealous. They cannot abide my beautiful colors magnified in the pool*, Siel scoffed.

Bending her head for a first lap, she caught a reflection of movement from above. A skyfall! WHOOSH! SLAM! A giant net knocked her down and covered her. Siel kicked; she flipped into the air; she tried to run; she jumped backwards, then threw her head up with a guttural scream.[†] More and more, Siel entangled herself in the net until she fell, whining piteously. Her beautiful fur could not save her from the trap.

"A young female cheetah!" the zoologists shouted. "What a beauty!" The animal scientists meant no harm to Siel. Their job was to capture and study animals in the wild. But Siel had never met zoologists before, and now she was afraid. The scientists pushed a dart into Siel's neck, a dart filled with sleep medicine. Siel felt only a prick, but the surprise made her yowl in anger. She tried to strike out with her paw, big as a baseball mitt, but it was heavy and clumsy.

The paw fell to the ground with a thud. Sleep was closing in on Siel, as had the dastardly net. She tried to growl again, but it was kitten-like, a tiny and tinny "meeeeoooow."

Siel, the cheetah, fell heavily into a drugged sleep. As the zoologists moved the cat to their laboratory, she dreamed she was a traveler. *I'm finally leaving this lonely scorched grassland,* she dreamed. *Now I'll show the whole world my purrrrfectly beautiful coat.*

SCRITCH-SCRATCH! There was a tickle under her chin. TAP-TAP! A pat on her shoulder. STROKE-STROKE! A neck massage. Siel dreamed that other animals were bumping into her and rubbing close to admire her... *or maybe an entire tribe of humans is lining up to pet my coat!* She wondered.

Actually, the zoologists were gently probing Siel's limbs, her tummy, her coat, discussing her age, her possible activities in the grasslands. And yes, they were commenting on her wonderful coloring.

FLASH! FLASH! Siel dreamed that her fans and even news reporters were now taking pictures of her dazzling speckled coat. *I've been discovered! The whole world will fall in love with me!* She dreamed. The zoologists continued taking many pictures and quietly discussed their findings.

CLACK! CLINK! Siel heard the sound like a bell inside her head but felt pressure on her lips and gums. She dreamed that she was about to be served a big feast. She tried to move her thick pink tongue but she only drooled into her ear. The zoologists were not about to feed her, but rather they were checking her mouth and counting her teeth.

ZIP! ZAP! The zoologists measured her long twitchy tail and her round padded paws. She felt her retractable[†] claws being squeezed in and out of her paws. She dreamed she was going to show off her incredible speed by digging into the ground at the start. Surely, if the world wasn't completely mesmerized[†] by her stunning showy hide, she thought, they must be wowed by the fact that she and her cheetah cousins are the fastest of all land animals in the world.

But what's this? Siel wondered. Someone was gently fastening a collar around her neck. This band held a type of computer that would allow the zoologists to study Siel when she went back to the savanna. The band would not get tangled and would not hurt her. She began to pant. She began to smile. Now wait a minute… Siel is a cheetah and we can't be sure that she smiles, right? But, she did feel very excited. She dreamed that she had become someone's beloved pet! *A collar means I belong to someone. Someone to be my Friend!* Siel thought.

Oh, how very proud she was! *Purrrrrrrrrrrrr! My most marvelous coat has attracted someone to love me! What a lucky cheetah I am! What a beautiful cat I am!* Siel was so happy that she rolled to her back and danced with her great paws in the air. One zoologist scratched her buff[†] belly. They all chuckled.

From somewhere Siel heard laughing and felt the belly rubs. She imagined this was her very own Someone.

∽∽∽

Days later Siel awoke in her familiar grasslands. For hours she followed her usual paths to get food and drink. She didn't swagger. She didn't brag. She passed the other animals haughtily,[†] but inside she felt heavy, unsettled, lonely. She didn't know why. She walked and wondered. She wandered and wondered.

By the time Siel returned to her fragrant spot at the base of her favorite acacia umbrella tree she could remember only scraps of her dreams. Her thoughts seemed fuzzy and unreal. But her collar was real. She scratched at the strange stricture[†] on her neck.

She sniffed the air for human scents with her grand nose. She squinted her golden eyes to look for unfamiliar movements. Satisfied that she was alone, Siel licked her pretty

flanks[†] with long wet strokes. The fiery sun was sneaking through the tree tops and making her tired head heavy. She slowed licking until she could barely pull her tongue back into her mouth. Her eyes hung droopy; her tongue lay lazily on her bottom teeth. She breathed in tiny slow sniffs. Her head nodded.

Suddenly, a BANG-CRASH split her slumber. All four paws full of claws dug into the ground and she hunched, ready to strike. Her body was stiff and still; her muscles were hard as rocks. She slowly peered from side to side but moving only her eyes. She anticipated more commotion. Another

BANG-CRASH told Siel that something was approaching from the direction of the long stand of thorny trees in the north. People again? Siel wondered.

She crept to the edge of the treeline, one paw tip-toeing after the other, one after the other, one after the other. She heard yet another BANG-CRASH and saw a plume of dark smoke. An old open-air Jeep was back-firing and popping along a dirt path through the grasslands. Siel had seen safari guides zoom by before in their Jeeps. And, she had watched afar as "lazy lookers," she called them, came to safari. These visitors always chattered loudly, interrupting her various daily naps.

But no safari Jeep had been this noisy before. It was spilling oil, and the driver kept jerking the steering wheel. And no lazy-looker crowd had ever been so irritating to Siel. The sharp sun struck the windshield and reflected into the cat's eyes. She blinked hard and jerked her head aside.

"Look here! Oh, look there!" The tour guide was pointing and shouting to his passengers. The four other people in the Jeep were trying to share one pair of binoculars. Each one tried to look here, look there, look everywhere before his or her turn was over. Arguments ensued. BANG-CRASH sputtered the Jeep as it zig-zagged along. And then, it slowed to a crawl.

Siel snickered. They will never see me in my perfect camouflage, she bragged with contempt. She was about to turn back to her napping spot when she spied a girl sitting in the back seat of the Jeep. The girl held an umbrella over her head. The umbrella was a blood-red color with tassels dangling all around the edge. A book was open on the girl's lap. The girl shifted her eyes from the commotion around her and instantly looked right into Siel's eyes. Again, Siel felt a stab in her eyes, but this time it was not the sun. It was the girl's own knowing eyes staring at Siel, large as quarters, deep as the waterhole, dark as shining ebony. The girl with the umbrella leaned forward from the railing of the Jeep. She stared and stared.

Siel had seen many humans, but few had ever seen her. And no one at all had ever looked into Siel's eyes! These riots of color, Siel's eyes were a kaleidoscope of green golds, tawny yellows, purple blacks, and even shifting shades of blue, like cut crystals spinning on a string, cat eyes that could hypnotize and even distract from the marvelous cheetah coat. Has anyone ever seen eyes like this before? Even the zoologists who had petted Siel's face and inspected her eyes, even they could not see deep into Siel's soul. No one had ever seen Siel's soul...until now.

☞☞☞

The green and brown scrubland had always been safe for Siel. But now she felt locked to the girl's stare as the Jeep rambled on. Instinctively[†] Siel crept backwards. Still, the girl stared. Suddenly the girl stood up and grabbed the Jeep's side railing. She squealed and stuttered, "LOOK! L-L-LOOK! A Chee...A Cheee..." but the adults were too busy arguing. They didn't hear the girl. They didn't notice Siel.

When the girl jumped up, the book fell from her lap, bumped on the edge of the Jeep, and flipped into the tall dry grass. The girl didn't notice, but Siel did. Siel allowed barely a glance at the book, but immediately her eyes were pulled back to the girl's like a paddle ball on an elastic string. Time seemed to stand still. Siel saw in slow motion the girl rotating her head and body to stare, stare, stare into Siel's eyes. Dreamily, Siel noticed the Jeep spitting dust and smoke hiding the eyes of the one from the other.

Siel sat hard with a thud. She stared after the disappearing Jeep. The orange sun silhouetted, then swallowed the scene. Siel imagined how the girl's soft hand might stroke her neck, pat her head, gently, gently, gently. The imagination was so strong that Siel thought perhaps the touch was real. Siel shivered…twice. She felt dazed. She plodded back to her umbrella tree. Siel lay down, heart pounding. She could hardly move until nightfall.

Who was that girl? What was that look? The lonely cheetah wondered over and over.

In the bright creamy moonlight Siel ambled down the Jeep path toward the book. She circled the book cautiously. The title was *The Winds of the Earth.* But Siel doesn't read, you know. She is a cheetah.

Siel sniffed the book, nostrils wide. She nudged the book with a curled paw. She jumped backed a bit to see if this thing would move on its own. She reared up and pounced on the book. She licked the cover. She nibbled the edge. She hooked the book cover with a long sharp claw and flipped it open. She saw this,

JULIA

But Siel couldn't read it. So she hooked the book again and tossed it up, up into the air. She grabbed the book with her teeth and shook her head. Siel played and played like a kitten with a ball of string. In an hour, the book lay in pieces of hard-bound cover and torn pages. While having all this fun, Siel wondered what the book could mean to the girl. Siel sat and panted.

Clouds darkened the moon and rough breezes stirred the papers off the ground. Siel got excited again and jumped to catch a lifting shred here and there. Her flat tail swatted several pages off the ground, and they, too, took flight in the wind. After a long evening, Siel tired of her game. She returned to her sleeping spot. But her head still felt fuzzy with recurring curiosity and amazement. *That look! The book!*

Wild winds kicked up, rattling and whistling through treetops and shrubs. Straw grasses, taller-than-you, blew over. Thorny dry branches bent and snapped. Savanna animals smelled the storm and scurried to find cave and rock structures to stay safe for the night. The beasts whinnied and bawled and barked. They understood the ever-present danger of lightning setting the prairies afire. That is the way of nature in the grasslands. But Siel didn't scurry and she didn't worry. She could only ponder again and again and again the staring girl with the blood-red umbrella.

めめめ

The scatterings of *The Winds of the Earth* lifted on the hot harsh night breezes in the Serengeti. Pieces and pages blew all around, shuffling through underbrush and stabbing sharp sticks. Up, up, higher and farther the winds blew the book remains out of Africa and beyond. Papers twirled and swirled, danced and darted, glided and slid for days and then months all around the Earth on worldwide wind currents. (Did you think I was going to say the worldwide web? Ha!). How long do you think it might take a scrap of paper to flip and fly and blow around the whole world?

The world's winds finally spent themselves in months of flurry around continents and nations. Currents calmed like air escaping from a pricked balloon. Book pieces sprinkled down like confetti. Some fell in schoolyards, on rooftops, in city parks, on farms, in open car windows, in shopping mall parking lots, on business plazas all around the world, in deserts and lakes, mountains and glaciers. It seemed everyone, everywhere got a piece of the book *The Winds of the Earth*. Did you find one?

In a land far, far away from Siel, there lived a young woman named Julia. She drove into her family's driveway where a smattering of white confetti in the yard caught her eye. Curious, she parked and sprinted over the lawn. Close up, she saw that it was actually larger than confetti. It was a wickedly wrinkled piece of paper. She dropped to her knees and smoothed the page with her hands. There was a picture. Suddenly, Julia thought she recognized something in the picture. She was stunned. She stared, stared, and stared. She grabbed the paper and ran into the house yelling, "Mom,

Mom! Look at what I found in the driveway! Where did this come from?"

"What, Julia? Where are you?" Mom called tracing through a couple of rooms toward Julia's voice.

"Mom, look at this page. It's a lot like one from the book I lost while we were on safari. Remember, Mom?"

"There you are, honey. Now, what? Stop dancing around, Julia."

"Mom, the safari! Remember the book I was reading? I was what? Ten, maybe twelve, at the time? Yesssss! That book! I dropped it in the grasslands…"

"Of course, I remember the safari, honey, but…"

"How I loved that safari! The animals! That cheetah!" Julia's eyes were shining at the memories.

Mom became distracted starting supper, but still tried to engage her daughter's conversation, "Well, honey, you've said that our African safari was the very reason you are studying zoology in college this semester…"

"Oh, Mother, listen! That book I had…what was the title?"

"Well…uhh, the book? Uh…"

"Oh! I remember!" Julia went on. "It was titled *The Winds of the Earth*. Look at this picture! It's the manager on a wind farm from that book…I know it's from that very book…"

"Well…it could be, but, how?"

"Mom, focus! Look at the farmer's rubber boots in this picture. They were muddy brown in my book.

In this picture the farmer's boots are such a beautiful cheetah design! How can that be?"

"Oh, yes, I see, honey, but how can you be sure this page is from…"

"And…and…oh! It was that Jeep we rode in…my book fell…!" Julia's excitement drove her on in this basically one-sided conversation, "…but, oh my goodness! Is this weird or what? I dropped my book on safari EXACTLY at the spot I saw that cheetah…that gorgeous little cheetah. Do you remember, Mom?"

"Uhh…did we see a cheetah, dear?"

"Doesn't matter…look at the picture again, Mom. These cheetah design boots! They are awesome! Where did this farmer get such boots? Wonder if I could buy some?"

Every single page, every piece of a page that had flown around the Earth had a picture with someone sporting[†] cheetah design. There were hundreds and hundreds and hundreds of pictures:

- a glider plane pilot, her cheetah print scarf flying in the wind
- a teenager clutching her cheetah print backpack on a windy school day
- an islander, his cheetah print FLIPPITY-FLAPPITY flip-flops running for shelter during a storm
- a mom with cheetah print house slippers hopping to the mailbox in an autumn gust
- a tribal chieftain wrapped up in his cheetah print robe, desert sands swirling
- sheer cheetah print curtains in an elegant high rise apartment, billowing in a breeze

Do you have any item in cheetah print? How many different ways can you imagine using cheetah designs? Well, it seemed that people from the Four Winds had fallen in love with cheetah print! Everyone who saw it wanted to wear cheetah design or decorate with it. Fashion designers and manufacturers around the world quickly copied and created businesses producing cheetah design clothing and products.

One day the European Zoological Association (EZA)[†] noticed the phenomenal[†] fashion trend. Curious because of their love and respect for all animals, EZA members began to discuss cheetah fashion. The lead scientist drew the striking similarities in the thousands of cheetah patterns they reviewed: blacks, browns, tans, yellows, oranges in irregular spots, dark on light background. "Is it possible," she asked her team, "that there might be one cheetah somewhere in the world whose Joseph's Coat has actually inspired this industry?" The association took the query to task[†] by gathering all the data of cheetahs tracked around the world.

Soon, the news broke that, indeed, there had been one elusive little cheetah in the Serengeti that was the inspiration for the fashion trend of the decade! Of course, you know that it was Siel's beautiful coat that was copied all around the world. But Siel didn't know these things. After all, she is just a cheetah and she doesn't read the news, remember?

The long ago moonlit night that stirred up the hot storm that scattered *The Winds of the Earth* was only a distant memory for Siel. Through the seasons, Siel still swaggered from her thorny tree to the waterhole to the lookout boulder to the soft grassy napping places. She raced after her prey; she ate well and slept a lot. She still obsessively[†] groomed her coat, her most prized possession.

But over the years, Siel had grown irritated with humans bothering her savanna. They came to study animals or put up ranch fences, drilling and plowing, building and invading. Siel felt penned in. She still had not made friends with the too-tall giraffes or the too-round elephants or the too-loud hyenas. She was a loner...and lonely.

The zoologists returned infrequently to change her computer collar. She no longer growled at them nor was afraid really; however, she still had to be tricked into the net for her capture. She was still a wild...and irritable cat! But her visits with the zoologists always renewed Siel's dream— the one in which she finds someone who becomes her very own friend, a friend who would look into her shining eyes and see her soul.

It never seemed to grow old. Siel so often tried to piece together a few bits of the dusty thoughts left over from the long-ago dreams: the chin tickles, the head pats, the shoulder rubs...and that girl who stared into Siel's eyes. No, no! Not the scientists! With all their looking, they never found Siel's soul. But she still dreamed of One who once did.

Siel panted after her morning meal and noticed the droning sound of a little biplane overhead. It was like the sound of the bothersome flies around her face. A jackal bawled in the brush wanting to pick at the leftovers of Siel's meal. Why not? Siel capitulated.[†] I'm full. But just to assert her dominance, Siel rose and growled at the brush. The jackal whinnied in fear and Siel chuckled...a sort of cheap cheetah chuckle.

The biplane had flown in circles overhead like the buzzards waiting for Siel to leave the hunting grounds. As Siel plodded toward the greener grasses, she left the buzzards behind, but the biplane seemed to follow her. Her full belly and the droning sounds made Siel sleepier than ever. But perhaps she wasn't just tired. She was feeling old. Siel conceded,[†] *I'm tired, old, and lonely. But still beautiful… always beautiful.* And then Siel dozed.

∾∾∾

The giant sun glared. It shot through a squat leaning tree throwing only a bit of shade over Siel. She awoke and leaned into the shade like a snake retreating under a rock. She noticed the droning of the biplane was gone and the flies were now biting her underparts. Her twitchy tail swatted the short grasses into submission like a jump rope slapping your playground gravel. A cooling breeze twisted the red and golden grass heads on their toothpick stems, and their shadows scurried across Siel's face. But Siel didn't scurry. She barely blinked. She lay long and stretched out like a quilt tossed off your bed. Her rough pink tongue like a kitchen sponge groomed every inch of her Joseph's Coat of Many Colors: black spots on a background of light browns, yellows, tans, and streaks of orange. She preened until sunspots of gold shone from her fur.

Suddenly, a BANG-CRASH split the air. Although bored with "people noises," Siel couldn't go back to preening. Something stirred inside Siel—a strange curiosity, a magnetic befuddling. Her dream resurfaced and a long-ago memory stirred. *Those eyes! That girl!* Siel felt her widening eyes glaze over as if in a trance. She shook her great head to clear her thoughts. She scratched at the collar. She imagined a slow gentle stroke down her neck. It felt so real that Siel was startled. She jumped up. *What am I feeling? What is happening to me?*

BANG-CRASH! Siel felt pulled toward the noise. She crept expectantly toward the edge of tall green grasses. There puttered a noisy Jeep. There rode a zoologist. This is the world's most famous zoologist, the one who always carries an umbrella over her head, a blood-red umbrella with tassels dangling all around the edge. But Siel knows nothing about fame, neither Julia's nor her own. Siel is just an elusive little cheetah, remember?

The Jeep stops. Two pairs of eyes stare as sunshine explodes around them. Ebony in kaleidoscope. Julia smiles and raises an inviting hand. Siel stands tall in the grass, then steps forward, out of the scrub. Siel bows her head low, awaiting the touch of her Someone.

Perhaps dreams can come true when you throw your spots in the wind...

Glossary and Story Questions

Siel is our little cheetah's name, pronounced "see yell." You try it. This word means "soul" in the Afrikaans language (a Low Franconian West Germanic language descended from Dutch). Afrikaans is a colonial and now, minority language, in South Africa, in and around the independent nation of Namibia. Although our cheetah, Siel, currently roams the Serengeti which is located in middle and eastern Africa, her name is in honor of the Cheetah Conservation Fund (CCF) with headquarters in Namibia. And, in addition, Siel's name is a reference to the author's home state (Ohio), The Cincinnati Zoo and Botanical Gardens which through their Angel Fund helped to establish the CCF in 1994.

The CCF is an internationally recognized center of excellence for the preservation of endangered cheetahs (only about 7,000 left in the world!) and protection of their ecosystems. Botswana and Australia also headquarter chapters of the CCF.

Submission means to obey or to put yourself in agreement with someone or something. The term may be displayed in a position of bowing down. A cheetah's tail is long but somewhat flat. It is like a rudder on a boat and helps the cheetah steer or guide her direction as she runs so fast… up to 70 mph (113 km/h). When she swings her tail she swats the tall grasses. The grasses would bend over and may lay flat in a position, suggesting the act of submission.

Savanna is a "biome" or a particular arrangement of

land, weather, plants, and animals on Earth. A savanna is rolling land with short and tall grasses, and a few scrub trees and is often a transition land between a tropical rainforest and desert (two other biomes). The weather is warm all year around, sometimes very hot and dry (winter) and sometimes very wet and humid (summer). Large herds of big and smaller hoofed animals graze continually on grasses. And other animals are meat-eaters and chase the grass-eaters. Siel is an animal of prey. She may eat jackal, antelope, rabbits, and gazelle.

Describe the biome in which you live.

Acacia Tree is a typical and symbolic tree of African grasslands. It is a small tree, shorter than 40 feet. It may be flat-topped with spiky, spiny branches holding up just a few tufts of leaves which are shaped like ferns. Large birds may roost in flat-topped acacias. Or the tree may have a gracefully curving trunk with numerous winding branches and ending in an umbrella-shaped top full of dangling ferns. Lions are often photographed resting on the branches of the acacia tree. The tree may be thorny and seasonally bears white flowers and long brown pods full of seeds. Some Bible scholars believe that the very tough and enduring wood of the acacia tree may have been the wood used to build the tabernacle that God designed and instructed the Israelites to build some 3,000 to 4,000 years ago (Exodus 36-39).

What do you think the term "merciful tree" means?

Name a tree that is typical of the Deep South United States. Name a tree that is typical of where you live.

Serengeti is a word that applies generally to the vast

grasslands of middle and eastern Africa but is also the name of the national park in the country Tanzania. The Serengeti is the most popular place in Africa for safaris. The original peoples, the Maasai, called their herding/grazing grounds "the place where the land runs on forever." If you could name your own neighborhood, what would you call it?

Joseph's Coat of Many Colors refers to the Bible story, Genesis 37, of the shepherd boy Joseph, whose father, Jacob, made him a very beautiful and expensive tunic of many colors. Joseph was proud of his coat and bragged that he was loved best by his father. This caused a lot of trouble for Joseph. However, Joseph was a man chosen by God, and he became one of the most powerful and blessed men on Earth. Does this give you any ideas where Siel's bragging might lead her?

Preen means that Siel licked her fur while wearing a big smile because she was so proud of her beautiful coat! Have you ever finished dressing up for a special event and smiled at yourself in the mirror? Yes, you have!!

Swagger is a lazy and sassy walk. Siel swung her hindquarters, plodding carelessly. Anyone watching would see that she was confident and uncaring about who was around her.

Guttural Scream Siel cried out in a low choking growl that ended in a high-pitched scream of agony. Have you ever heard a violent, horrible scream on TV or on a roller coaster or at some fright or tragedy? Once you hear it, you never forget it.

Retractable Claws Just like on your cat, claws may be squeezed in and out by gently pressing on the foot pads. But your cat does not have the sharp and giant claws that Siel has. Siel uses her claws to dig deeply into the ground like shoes with cleats give traction to the football player for starts, stops, and turns on a dirt field. Siel's claws give her an immediate start to chase her supper and allow her to turn suddenly and sharply in the pursuit.

Mesmerized Siel is bragging again, even in her dreams. She imagines that anyone in the world who saw her would be so captivated and fascinated that they would stare at her and be unable to look at or think about anything else. Can you think of anything you've seen that not only gave you a "double-take" but also held your attention, even if you wanted to look away? If so, then you were mesmerized.

Buff The definition used in this story is a yellowish-beige color. Animals and birds often have underbellies that are lighter color than their backs or upper coloring. In addition, the underbellies often have softer, downy fur as opposed to stiffer, course hairs of the hide or backs of animals.

Find two other meanings of the word "buff."

Haughtily means behaving as if you think you are better than others; arrogant, uppity, prideful, although by this point in the story, Siel's heart is not in her bragging anymore.

Stricture means something that feels tightly attached, perhaps not hurtful but noticeable or irritable, like a tight sweater around your neck or a jacket cuff that binds your wrist. Name a piece of clothing that may be "restrictive" for you.

Flanks are an animal's smooth hips or top of the hind legs; the rump.

Instinctively means (automatically) doing something without planning or having to figure it out. Usually it is something you do automatically while focusing on something else. This is also a safety response that your body does for you like closing your eyes at a bright flash, covering your ears at a loud blast, or putting up your hands to protect the front of your body when something or someone comes too close too quickly toward you.

Sporting may simply mean wearing something, but it often means making a show of what you are wearing. Perhaps many of the "models" in the pictures from *The Winds of the Earth* were actually participating in activities having to do with wind education (topics in that book), but also they were showing off their cheetah print. Mysterious!!

European Zoological Association is a fictional name for an organization that studies and protects animals. Who do you think might be the lead scientist?

The International Society of Zoological Sciences headquartered in Beijing, China, is a real association that supports education about animal studies, publishes a scientific journal, posts regular blogs of zoological interest for the public, and hosts conventions called a congress in places around the world to benefit wildlife conservation. They also sponsor a "Young Zoologist Award." Two interesting blog posts are titled (1) "Supersniffer mice could one day detect land mines diseases" and (2) "Why birds don't need exercise to stay fit for epic flights."

The Zoological Association of America (ZAA) is also real, headquartered in Punta Gorda, Florida. With a three-pronged core mission, the ZAA accredits professional zoological facilities, promotes animal conservation, and provides a variety of educational and research events including an annual convention since at least 2005 in a variety of places around the United States and frequent workshops. They promote animal ambassador programs and classroom education while cooperating with other zoological entities around the whole world.

Phenomenal means highly remarkable! I found at least 10 synonyms for this word. Can you search synonyms and write some down?

Can you think of a fad, a fashion, or a trend which is phenomenal right now, or list a person you think is phenomenal?

Query to Task means turning a question into a project or job. The zoological team turned a simple question into an actual project. Then, they researched until they found an answer. What topics have you been curious about? Have you researched to find out more?

Obsessively means focusing on and repeating a behavior over and over and over again, unnecessarily and to the extreme. And so, dirty or not, Siel licked her coat, day and night, to keep it shining and in prime condition…and hoping others would notice and admire her.

Capitulated means giving up or simply not bothering to resist an opponent.

Conceded means that Siel admitted to herself something is true (she was getting older), even though she'd prefer to deny it.

Early in the story there's **foreshadowing** of Siel's loneliness. It fills nearly a whole chapter. Describe this.

Circle all the references to "**light**" that you can find. There are no less than 30!

Tracking Big Cat

for Simon

"**S**am, come help find the cat; please, oh, please, dear boy!" Yeah, that's how my Grandma talks! But she certainly did sound close to tears. You know how emotional grandmas can be. But I'd give my life to make my Grandma happy…and, I almost did!

I have to say, this WAS pretty serious. It was her last cat left. Grandma used to have a dozen cats for the barns and at least two in the house for company. But…well, lots of stuff can happen to cats, you know. Some cats ran off, some fought with raccoons…and lost. Last year, neighbors told Grandma they would be putting out poisons and traps to clean the "riff-raff" out of the neighborhood. It seems they were trying to protect their own gardens and farms after a season of being overrun by mice, rats, stray cats, coons, and other "four-leggers," as Grandma calls them. Those lumbering, digging, chewing creatures didn't bother her, or so she says, but, of course, she stays inside almost always nowadays, so very little that goes on outdoors bothers her. But the neighbors had had enough.

And so, poor ol' cats! There hadn't been any grain in Grandma's big barn since…well, before Grandpa passed away when I was a little kid. The mice got hungry and moved away. And the cats left behind were kinda starving anyway. When any barn cats did go out hunting, most of them got tangled up with the neighbors' pest control efforts. I think I saw one or two skittish cats whizzing through the barn just last week, but they had to be squatters.[†]

Grandma's house cat is a prize Chartreux.[†] Really! He won a prize at some famous cat show. His coat is thick as June grass. He's as heavy as two one-gallon milk jugs. And his whiskers are as long as coffee stirrers. His coloring is silver-charcoal with occasional single white hairs…not white spots, mind you…just a single brilliantly white hair here and there! His eyes are usually dark orange, but in certain lights, they glow like gold. He sure is a big, beautiful cat. And his name is…"Big Cat." Yeah, creative name, right?

So, here's how THAT happened: When I was about five I guess, I was visiting Grandma. She took me along to pick out her latest cat addition. We brought home this very fat, soft grey kitten. I suggested the name "Shadow." Don't you think that's a cool name? Grandma didn't.

"Oh no, dear grandson. Look at the giant paws on this little boy. He's going to grow up to be a lion of a cat!" So, she named him "Big Cat." Surprise! He's been Grandma's prize boy for years.

Big Cat took a liking to me immediately. Grandma became his mommy and I was his daddy. Yeah, it's weird. He is really a good cat and loves being inside and right beside Grandma…or me. When strangers or even my cousins come by, Big Cat doesn't scratch or bite or hiss, like some cats do. But he does stick up his very tall tail and walk away from anyone…except Grandma…or me, like I said.

Big Cat has never really gone missing before, but he does like to mosey[†] around outside in the yard and under bushes. However, he doesn't hang around the barn very often. He's always made it very clear that he is in a class much higher than the ill-bred[†] barn cats. If any of them ever wandered toward the house, Big Cat would give them "the tail" and would walk regally to the back porch with his Cheshire[†] nose in the air. He'd sit there proud and stiff as a board until Grandma came to the door to call him in. No other cat ever got past him.

"Why did you answer the phone, Sam? Are you sick? Did you not attend school today?" Grandma now sounded worried about me when she realized it was a school day.

"No, Grandma, school is canceled; wind chill today made it too cold. Listen, I can come over, but I'll have to have Mom drop me off instead of riding my bike."

"Of course, of course, Son, but…but…oh, please excuse me for stuttering, but, well…" she was trying so hard to not sound pushy, "When...I mean, how soon do you plan, well...? Ohhh, where can my Big Cat be? Where's my boooooyyyy?"

"Don't worry, Grandma. We're putting on coats right now!"

Mom told me, "She'll probably nap as soon as you find Big Cat, Sam, so go ahead and take your Kidzgo game." Mom reminded me to play quietly while Grandma sleeps. *Well, of course, Mom,* I thought, *I'm always quiet when somebody's sleeping!* Why do parents always tell you stuff you already know?

So, you've probably heard about a Kidzgo, right? Well, Grandma got the game piece for me for Christmas last year, but she isn't fond of me playing on it. She said, "I know you wanted this toy, Sam, and you know it is all my pleasure to provide suitable games and pastimes for you, but, my darling, I certainly don't want you to 'lose your brains' by playing on it all the time." Grandma says, "lose your brains" for anything she thinks is silly or dumb. "Just give your thumbs a bit of a rest, and instead of Kidzgo play Rummy with me."

Anyway, Mom said she'd pick up some supper after work and we would eat with Grandma. Then, Mom ruined my whole day! "Sam, we'll have to get you to the tub and then early to bed tonight. You have fifth grade state tests at school tomorrow!" *Snow,* I started praying, *please let there be a lot of snow or beautiful, bitter cold!* I'm not picky in my prayers, just hoping to get out of state testing.

"I walked all over the house and looked 'everwear, everwear,' I tell you!" Grandma said before we even got inside her door. However, Grandma doesn't see well and no longer goes up the stairs nor down to the basement! So I guess it will be my job to look "everwear." Even if Grandma had been able to tromp upstairs or down to the basement, she probably couldn't see Big Cat skittering all around like a shadow, unless he stopped at her feet and rubbed her ankles.

So Mom dropped me off, and I made a quick round through the main floor of the house looking in all Big Cat's usual hiding and napping places. Grandma and I checked the cat food dish. It looked like there hadn't been even a nibble. The bowl was rounded with food and Grandma said she filled it last night before she went to bed. She couldn't remember if Big Cat had jumped up on her bed through the night or not.

I was ready to stick my head outside to look around when Grandma said, "Sam, I know the habits of my Big Cat. Twice daily, he's regular. I know he uses, uhmm, goes to, well, the litter box... *No, Grandma,* I thought, *please don't ask; don't say it!* ...

"...you understand me, Son? Will you look into the litter box and sniff it for me? Now...I regret I must ask, but I can't bend..."

"Yeah, yeah, yeah, I know, Grandma," I said as sweetly as I could with gritted teeth. "Don't worry about it." UHHHHHG! Have you ever done it? Have you ever investigated a litter box?

But, I have to say, fresh cat litter is...well...fresh! So... now we had three big clues that Big Cat had probably been out of the house for at least a day:

(1) Grandma hasn't seen him nor petted him
(2) food untouched and
(3) litter box clean

Mom had told me to stay inside because of the brutal

cold. So I helped Grandma walk to every window and look out…or, that is, I looked out and told her everything I saw. It was amazing how well she knew her farmyard even though she couldn't see it.

"First thing, Sam, look out across our bountiful front yard rolling gently to the road. Then, sweep your eyes along the edges of the road…as far as you can see, Son. Is there anything gray…?" Grandma's throat caught and she sniffed.

"I'm looking, Grandma." What should I say? Even if Big Cat *was* smashed on the road, I wouldn't have been able to see it from here. Everything was gray! It had been getting grayer, hazier all morning. *The temp might be going up but the fog and precip are comin' in!* I thought. "I don't see anything, Grandma. Let's look out the back windows. Big Cat loves to slip under your shed or sleep in the peach tree. Since it's so cold, he might have even darted to the barn." We didn't see Big Cat but Grandma felt hopeful when I mentioned the barn. "Brilliant, Sam! That's a warm hiding spot for my Big Cat, isn't it?"

After checking a few more first floor windows without spying the cat, we made peanut butter and banana sandwiches for a brunch. Grandma was talking about a snowstorm on the farm years ago, "…the sun had dropped behind the barn roof and just like that…" Here, she snapped her bent, arthritic fingers, "…the world went from glorious, heavenly brightness to snow-bitten yellows to swirling pale grays…" And here, Grandma swirled the butter knife in circles in the air, "…and finally the sky darkened to a sea of gravel." And she stabbed the knife back into the family-sized peanut butter jar. I couldn't laugh. I was too stunned by Grandma's dramatic act!

When Grandma got out a large double-bottomed saucepan and the five-pound bag of organic cocoa powder, I knew she was making me the Drink of Kings![†] First, she dumped the cocoa into the pan, and a plume of soft brown powder fluffed into the air. Then she poured a lot of crystal white sparkly sugar into the pan. She whisked the dry ingredients and added chopped butter over medium heat. She asked me to whisk while the butter melted and turned the whole mess into a chocolate sea. She slowly poured in a half gallon of whole milk, continuing to whisk while I sprinkled in just a shake each of cayenne pepper and cinnamon.

"Remember, Sam," Grandma warns EVERY SINGLE TIME we make this drink, "We must take it off the heat immediately when tiny bubbles appear around the top of the liquid. Do not ever..."

"Never let it boil, Grandma. I got it!"

Then we chop the giant marshmallows into small pieces and dip them into the steaming drink. We like them to melt on the top of the hot cocoa rather than let them bob against our lips while we drink. This is the mostest bestest, thickest, darkest, sweetest, smoothest winter drink... fit for kings!

I tidied up the kitchen and convinced Grandma to take a nap while I checked the rest of the house for Big Cat. I stuck my head out the back door and called, "Kitty, kitty, kit..." Well, I'm sure you know how to call a cat. My nose instantly stung with cold. I squinted my eyes to see as far as I could, straining my eyes and brain to see through the bright haze. I thought I saw some movement just beside the door of the old white barn, but, like I said...hazy. Then, I thought I saw the tall ornamental grass patch vibrating like it does when Big Cat sprays it—marking his territory.[†] You know tomcats!

I blew warm breath into my cupped hands and covered my nose. I stared at the grass for some time while a little snow squall picked up. But I guess the icy breeze could account for the grass shaking. Regardless, no cat exited the patch.

Inside I took one more brief walk around the main floor, checking Big Cat's favorite hangouts: under the chairs and behind the sofa. Then, upstairs, I looked in every closet and peeked out every window. I even wiped my finger across ledges and furniture tops to see if there was cat hair, or just dust. I made a round of the dank basement and found nothing, except the little windows near the ceiling were collecting snow in the window well. *No Big Cat inside! Take a break*, I thought. It certainly did seem odd to not have him around, bumping into my ankles and stretching up my leg for a head scratch.

Back in the living room, I grabbed a quilt and plopped onto the couch with my Kidzgo to play *Superheroes Save the City*. Suddenly, I remembered a program I had never tried out before. It's called *Find It!* The application had a type of GPS and camera functions. It could be used to look for lost things by picture, by sound, and even by body heat sensor. It was supposed to work within a half-mile of point zero. I got real excited but nervous, too:

Could I figure out this application?

Did I have a picture of Big Cat to feed into the program?

Can I enter the sound of his meow or purr? (He is a very quiet cat.)

Yes, perhaps! I thought, my excitement mounting. I remembered a Kidzgo video I took of Big Cat playing with a ribbon with Grandma from Christmas Day. Big Cat did let out a yowl when Grandma stepped on his tail that day.

I watched a tutorial for *Find It!* and shared a snapshot from the video and Big Cat's yowl to the app. The screen lit up with diagrams like zooming street views of Google Earth. Although the pictures were a bit jerky and took time to load, I soon recognized our state, our town, and Grandma's farm. Incredible! The constant beeps, clicks, and tiny flashing lights were not helpful, but rather distracting to me. I tried to mute the game piece, but the app insisted on using the sound function as an integral part of the *Find It!* program.

The screen kept returning to the snapshot of Big Cat up on his back paws reaching for the ribbon. His head looked out of proportion...too big for his body, but it was definitely Big Cat. The app played his yowl every 30 seconds. That got annoying!

Every time the screen popped back to the GPS function, there was an icon of a hand with a pointing finger identifying a spot on Grandma's farm for half an instant, but then the hand swirled in a crazy circle or dimmed out completely. The screen switched back and forth from the big-headed cat picture and the silly yowl, to Grandma's farm, back to the cat, back to the farm. First, the finger pointed to the road in front of the farm, then it swirled out back to the barn. Another spin and the finger pointed to the front porch. Once the finger even seemed to touch the very top of the roof point of Grandma's farmhouse!

I grabbed my coat and boots while the Kidzgo seemed to be orienting. When I returned to the screen, Big Cat's face was huge, the recording of his yowl was constant, and the finger was steadily pointing! Either *Find It!* found it or I was on a wild goose chase (that is, a wild cat chase)!!

"Sam, I thought I heard Big Cat," Grandma said wearily as she came from her bedroom.

"Really? Where?" I jerked my head around, looking for Big Cat.

"Why, dear boy, have you donned your coat and boots?"

"Well...this game, Grandma...this app...pointing to, to, to..." Sam looked at the Kidzgo again, the finger on the screen steadily pointing to the barn.

"My stars, Sam! There it is again. Did you hear Big Cat?" I realized Grandma was hearing the yowling on the Kidzgo.

"Grandma, I gotta run out to the barn to check..."

"No, Sam!" Grandma nearly shouted. "It's not safe!"

"But the app, Grandma... the finger icon is pointing... look at this; I think I can find Big Cat in the barn..." Grandma's stern look made me stop blathering and glance out the window. Wow, was she right! Such little time had passed since I looked outside, and now I could barely see the barn. Even the giant oak tree which was halfway to the barn was sneaking about in snow swirls. The snow was blowing in tiny circles and then in cross hatches. The glittering flakes were tiny but caught the sun with every tilt, turn, and twirl. *Raining diamonds*, I thought. It was so beautiful but so powerful. Blinding! Freezing! I'll admit it...I shivered, but not from cold.

Then Grandma shocked me. She grabbed my hand and pulled me to the garage. "Put these on." There hung Grandpa's heavy brown Carhartt Bib Coveralls,[†] so I struggled into them, added a pair of wool socks and pulled my boots back on. Then, Grandma nodded her approval and took my hand again, leading me to the pantry. She pulled open the door and pointed to a top shelf. "Now pull that down, honey." There was a coil of rope big as a kitchen trash can. I reached high and tugged on the bottom of the coil. The whole thing came tumbling down on me. I was sitting on the floor covered with rope coils, and Grandma was laughing her hissing little laugh.

Quickly, she returned to her elegant but bossy voice, "Take the rope and tie it there, Sam." Grandma pointed to the light pole on the patio. "You see the oak tree?"

"Barely."

"Be sure the rope is tied tightly around the light pole. Then, carry the rope toward the oak tree. Walk all the way around the tree...just one time. Just one time, Sam. From there you should see the black iron garden gate...well, the gate may be blurred out by the snow, but the garden shed is just beyond the gate. The shed is bright red. Remember, we painted it Farm Fresh Red last summer? If your back is against the tree where the line of rope crosses, you will see the bright red between the gusts of snow and wind. Can you see it right now from here, my brave boy?"

"Yes, Grandma, There is a red streak that I see when the wind swirls the snow away."

"Leaving the tree and going to the shed will put you in a headwind, Love. You will be heading straight north and the wind will be in your face, Sam. You know that our coldest and fiercest weather comes from the north, yes? Walking north may be your biggest challenge, Son. Wear sunglasses to protect your eyes. When you finally get to the shed, you must go inside to take a break from the storm."

I was rehearsing Grandma's verbal map in my mind and looking in the general direction as she pointed. Grandma knew her farm so well and she was so devoted to Big Cat that I knew she would go out and do this on her own, if she were able. When I finally glanced at the Kidzgo again, nothing had changed. *Find It!* was saying that Big Cat had to be somewhere in that big barn. *This is crazy!* I thought. *Can a game piece app be real?*

Grandma continued her directions, "When you reach the black wrought iron[†] gate post, wrap your rope around it. It is attached to the shed. After you warm up in the shed, come out and back up against the gate with the shed on your right. On your right is north, remember? You will be facing due west. Walk straight west until you see the barn doors. If the snow hasn't stopped and the daylight fades, you will have to pay attention to putting one foot directly in front of the other, Sam. You have to go straight west long enough to see the barn.

"The sun will be dropping soon, so you should see at least a bit of extra brightness in the sky just above the barn roof. That might help you stay oriented to the west. Tie your rope to the barn door handles, then you'll have a rope path[†] back to the house."

I hope you don't think this is too uncool, but quite suddenly, Grandma pulled my face up and kissed both my cheeks! Then she nearly shouted in a cracking voice, "Wear your backpack to bring back Big Cat. Now, go get my baby!!" And she shoved me out the door!

Suddenly, my stomach got queasy and my eyes glazed over. I was thinking a million things at once:

What if the blizzard is really as bad as it looks?

Will the rope-walk work or will I get disoriented?

Could I die in this storm?

What if Big Cat isn't even in the barn…or what if he's dead?

Yeah, I was pretty nervous, but I have to say, I also felt very proud and happy. I knew Grandma really believed in me AND my Kidzgo. *Grandma's acting like I'm her knight in shining armor...that is, in heavy bib coveralls,* I thought with a little chuckle. I took a deep, scalding cold breath and wiped the tears from my eyes. Of course, the tears were naturally produced by the stinging cold. YOWL! The *Find It!* app was still repeating Big Cat's yowl. I was not looking forward to hearing that for the rest of the day!!

The light pole assignment was easy. Although I had to learn in a hurry how to manipulate the heavy rope and actually tie it with my bulky leather work gloves. I wrapped the rope twice and tied a fat knot, two of them! That would serve as my home base. As I walked away, the lantern at the top of the pole flickered three times and then stayed on, shining into the gathering dusk. I turned to see Grandma grinning and waving a good-bye. I knew the light switch was inside the back porch, right where she was standing. I gave her a thumb's up and set off toward the oak.

I was pretty excited and felt light on my feet, so I jogged toward the tree through crunchy snow two inches deep. I didn't jog for long! Heavy boots, a heavy coat, and Grandpa's sized 36 Carhartt made me feel like I was trapped in a space suit. In addition, my backpack stuffed with a flashlight and other explorer's items further weighed me down. As I ran, I nervously scanned the horizon to keep sight of the barn. Also, I kept glancing to my right for the red shed. My heartbeat began pounding in my ears, and I couldn't gulp enough breaths to keep my legs moving in rhythm. Suddenly, I thought I might puke. I slowed down and realized I couldn't move this quickly for the full 100 yards to the tree and then, beyond. I slowed slightly and ordered my brain, *Pace yourself, Sam, pace yourself.* I began to focus on just the oak tree ahead and one marching footfall at a time.

Soon the snowfall blocked my sight altogether of the barn, but the oak waved through the blurry white pattern of snow. When I finally reached the oak tree, I felt like celebrating and shouted, "I made it!" My happy grin dimmed as I remembered *this is just the first stop on this rescue mission*. So I concentrated on walking one time only around the tree, *One time, Sam, one time only*, Grandma had said. I looked down at my boot tracks and noted the snow was now over my ankle. Where the rope crossed around the trunk of the oak, I leaned my back against the bark and knew I was facing north. The blowing snow was not soft and fluffy, but stung my face like tiny needles. I pulled on my face mask and shoved the shafts of my sunglasses inside the hood of my coat. Looking north, I squinted for a sight of the shed. Looking right and left, I slowly moved my head. *Stop! There's a flash of red!* It was only an occasional streak, but I knew I saw it. I focused on that point and set out for the shed.

The *Find It!* app regularly emitted its recording of Big Cat's YOWL, but I got used to it like the tick-tock of an old grandfather clock in your living room. In short order, frozen snot crusted the rims of my nose and my eyebrows stung. I had to walk mostly with my head down, glancing up just enough to orient my footsteps toward the red streak. After a while, it seemed I was seeing the red streak fewer and fewer times I glanced up, even though I felt the wind receding and the snowflakes were getting bigger. *Am I losing orientation? Have I walked away from the shed?* A lump started up my throat and a knot in my stomach distracted me from my mission. I began to look to the right and to the left. *Where was the farmhouse? Was I close enough to see the big barn? Why isn't the big red shed showing up in my field of vision anymore?* My sunglasses fogged up as I began to breathe heavily, fear clawing at my spine. I jerked the sunglasses off to find a way to dry them…and there was the shed only 30 feet away! The dark tint of the sunglasses in the dimming light of early evening and the fog were all working together to block my vision. NOW was the time to sprint!

At the iron gate post, I wrapped the rope and made a loop knot. There was still plenty of rope so I threw the coil inside the shed and stumbled in myself, knocking over two rakes and a hoe. I pushed the door closed, as much as the rope would allow, and then scooted a 25-pound grass seed bag to hold the door. I flopped down on another seed bag and purposely slowed my breathing. I pulled off my gloves and massaged my fingertips, red as the shed. My nose finally warmed and began dripping snot all over my Grandpa's Carhartts. The vibration of the Kidzgo and the tinny YOWL that arose from my pants pocket acted like an alarm for me to get up and get going again. As I rose from the bag of grass seed, I noticed that the little bit of light left from the dropping sun, which I had enjoyed as I tramped to the shed, was now completely gone. It looked like a gravel sky.

Squinting south toward the oak tree, back from where I had come, I could see a tight line of rope coming out of "thin air" and tied to the post beside me. Even the bright beam from my flashlight disappeared into the murky swirling storm. I checked and tightened the knot and leaned my back against the iron post, the shed now on my right. I was facing west, or so Grandma had said. The air space in front of me was a dusky curtain allowing only ten steps of sight ahead. I walked ten steps and turned around. Yep! The shed was now out of sight! So, although I walked heel-to-toe straight ahead, there was really no way I could be certain what direction I was headed. White on every side! I began to walk in complete faith that there was a giant barn before me... somewhere.

Occasionally, I jerked at the rope behind me to see if I was still going straight west or if I had veered off course.

After a long march, I began feeling too warm, hungry, dazed, and even bored... if one can be bored surviving alone in a snowstorm!! It was a crazy feeling. And crazy gave way to fear. I began to think that it was very possible that I could become completely lost. *What if the rope broke? What if I've already wandered off the property? What if there is an unfrozen pond nearby into which I could fall?* Retelling this story to you, I guess those thoughts seem ridiculous, but in those lonely moments? I was spiraling downward in my thinking.

Suddenly, I felt a presence. Have you ever had anyone step up quietly behind you and without hearing a thing you just knew someone was there? That's the way I felt. *An angel? A devil? A person? Or something else?* I involuntarily yelled out, "Who's there?!" This was probably the first thing I had spoken aloud since I left the oak tree. My vocal chords were tight and my voice raspy. I turned my body all around and stared hard in every direction. Nothing. But I was sure I was not alone! Even shrouded in all that clothing, my insides felt it, my skin prickled, all my senses felt something, someone close by. I was startled and beyond disorientation. Once more, I strained my eyes, forcing them to look hard in every direction. As I stuck my head forward and brought up my arm in a salute to shield my eyes from the wind, my elbow struck hard against something. "OUCH!" I reached around to rub my elbow, and my other hand rammed into something solid. I tentatively reached out and touched the something. I tapped it, I knocked it, I banged on this presence. Raspy voice or not, I yelled, "THE BARN!!!!"

I used both my hands for my snow-blinded eyes to "see" all along the barn wall, to the south, to the north until I found the door. My clumsy gloves and the icy door handle gave me fits, but it finally opened to me. OK, here's another uncool thing, but, well, you would too: I cried! Yep, the Kidzgo was playing the disgusting YOWL and I was bawling! Inside, I slumped to my knees and berated myself for crying, but then I thanked God for this safe haven. My nose, eyes, and face began stinging right away. I pulled off my gloves and mask and scarf, wiped the warm palm of my hand across my face…my fingertips were stiff again and unfeeling. But I shoved on my gloves again to tie the last 20 feet of rope to the barn door handle, as Grandma instructed. *There! My rope path home!* I thought with dizzy joy.

The flashlight was weak. I used the last of the juice to glance around the dark barn, although I knew it pretty well. I stumbled to the bales of hay at the west, threw one off the pile and snuggled down between the small mountain of bales. I knew I should be looking and calling for Big Cat, but personal survival overtook my mission. In complete exhaustion, the warmth of the sweet hay sang me to sleep within seconds.

The YOWL from deep in my pocket once again acted as an alarm and roused me, but I just shuddered, stretched, and curled myself into a tighter ball to go right back to sleep. After drifting off, there was that yowl again. Oh! How I was hating that sound!! But suddenly I heard breathing in my ear and fuzzy tickles all over my face. I jerked my eyes open and felt more than saw a hairy head at my eye level. I screeched and jumped up. Then I heard a familiar but softened yowl —it was Big Cat himself...in the flesh!! "You WERE here all the time! My Kidzgo app found you, Big Cat!" I scooped him up and hugged him! *Mission accomplished!* I thought. I turned on my game's flashlight to look Big Cat over, "Are you hurt, Buddy? Just a little battle-weary, I suppose?" I sat back down and the cat hopped upon my lap. For a very long, quiet time I sat petting Big Cat and he warmed us both.

The howling winds had slowed, but I still heard a soft pelting against the barn doors. I heard other sounds, too: the swishing of a frayed rope hanging in the rafters, the rattling of old barn windows, a skittering rodent, and...and...faint meows? That is, I thought I heard a meow. *Is it that crazy Find It! app?* I wondered. "Well! I don't need you anymore," I said and snapped off the Kidzgo. Big Cat jumped off my lap and leapt over a couple bales of hay. He began sniffing and digging in one. "Hey, Buddy, what are you digging for? Let's get back on the road," I said.

I picked up Big Cat to insert him into the roomy backpack. But he wanted none of it. *This is going to be a rough walk home!* I thought. So, I tricked him. I opened a cat food packet and dumped it in the bottom of the backpack and laid it on the barn floor. He was famished, so Big Cat jumped right into the backpack. I began to zip it up, but out popped his head. Quick as a flash, he ran right back to his digging place in one of the hay bales. As I arose to go after him, I couldn't have guessed how many times I'd have to retrieve him and rearrange my backpack before we finally left the barn.

With my backpack fully loaded, I unlooped the rope from the barn doors and jogged gently but in complete confidence toward the shed. I wrapped the rope atop my shoulder and then under my arm, around and over my shoulder and under my arm, again and again. Although dusk had turned to a black night, the rope (and Big Cat, of course) was my constant companion. The rope path was my Eyes, my Light, my Hope, my Guide, my Friend, my Savior. I followed it faithfully gathering it to my chest as a holy thing. I passed the red shed, unlooped from the iron gatepost and gave a tug shouting out, "Hello, Oak Tree! Here we come!"

After some time of marching straight ahead to the south, the tree came into view. To my left I saw the farmhouse. Grandma told me later that Mom had left work early to come with supper, but they couldn't eat for worrying about me. Both Mom and Grandma had pulled rocking chairs to the back porch door and wrapped up in shawls, staring out

GLIMM, A GLIMPSE OF LIGHT FOUND

anxiously all through the dusky evening and into the black night. I was 50 feet from reaching the oak. I will remember forever the first instant I caught a glimpse of Mom and Grandma sitting there in their rocking chairs. I rose to my full five-foot height and waved crazily. Mom jumped up and stared toward the oak as if she could see me. But the porch light was throwing shadows against the blowing branches, only teasing her view. Her face was ecstatic with hope, but then she showed no recognition of me. So she sat back down.

When I finally reached the oak, I tried to jump up and down and wave my arms. "Surely you can see me now!" I yelled. It had to be a pitiful sight. I was trying to dance around, kicking snow into the air, but I felt like a zombie! My heavy snowsuit, the thickness of rope big as another head on my shoulder, the bulky, ever-moving backpack, all bouncing around with my little hops and waves. But…then suddenly, Mom saw me! She grabbed a blanket and stepped onto the patio and into the blowing wind. She waved the blanket and called for me. I couldn't hear her voice but saw her mouth yelling to me. Tears sprung to my eyes (yeah, real tears!), and I hurried toward her—I guess you could say I was hurrying, if one can hurry when he is fiercely dragging his body forward without feeling any of it! Soon, I felt a tent cover me and my mom's voice purring my name over and over and over again. She was crying and put her soft warm cheek against my icy one. We stumbled together to the patio. We both heard the most ugly "yeeeowllls" piercing the night, and I yelled over the winds, "Get this crazy thing off my back!"

In the warm kitchen I finally lay down my burden and stripped off my stiff clothes. Mom was holding my new *Batman, Return of the Caped Crusaders* pajamas, fresh from the dryer to put on. The wool socks, two pairs, also straight from the dryer felt the best. Grandma had warm cookies and her Kings' hot cocoa ready for me, but she was already hugging and kissing on Big Cat who had exploded from my backpack as soon as I laid it down. Her prized boy had a limp and a few cuts from prowling in the barn…and from other unexpected activities.

"So…Mom and Grandma! You'll never believe this adventure! Guess what Big Cat has been doing in the barn?" I was so eager to get out my story, but Big Cat yowled miserably and even swatted at Grandma's arms, although very gently. He demanded to be let down! He skittered across the slick floor to the backpack and clawed furiously at the opening.

I thought, *why tell the story when I can show them?* So I stooped to help Big Cat by further unzipping the opening of the backpack. We heard another louder yowl and out popped the head of a perfectly beautiful white furry cat. Her head glistened. I couldn't tell if the shine was from her sweaty ride in the backpack or just the brilliant glitter from each individual crystal hair on her pretty head. I smiled while Mom's mouth and Grandma's dropped wide open. *But,* I thought, *you ain't seen nothin' yet!* Wiggling at the tummy of this pure white Mrs. Big Cat were two tiny, eye-shuttered kittens. Big Cat lifted his tail and walked away from Mrs. Big Cat (probably because she's just an ill-bred barn cat, right?) But those kittens were obviously his babies. Big Cat had dug and dug in the barn until he had uncovered them to show them off to me.

Soooooooo…does this make me the kittens' grandpa? Weird!

Grandma and Mom both cried and exclaimed their surprise. While they began fussing over their plans for this new little family, I filled up on snacks.

"No, Mother," Mom said, "keeping the babies here is not a good idea. Think of all the work they will be for you... little fuzzballs under your feet all the time!"

Grandma said, "Oh you are right, honey. Can Sam keep them and bring them for visits?"

Mrs. Big Cat hissed loudly at all the attention, so I covered her and her babies with Grandma's shawl. I have to admit it, I felt every inch a hero! And, every inch exhausted!

At that moment...I don't think I had ever truly felt complete exhaustion before in my whole life! I left the kitchen and grabbed Grandma's feather-down quilt. I dropped like a bomb to the couch and just listened to my breath for a long time. I hadn't heard Big Cat follow me into the living room. So I started when he stood on his hind legs, reached to my face and softly batted my still-icy cheek. I'm guessing this was his "thank-you" for saving his life.

"Hi, Big Guy," I smiled and said softly. He jumped onto

my chest and walked the length of my body. After turning several circles at my feet, he curled into a ball and began to purr…actually, it was so loud, it became a snore and vibrated my feet like a massage. I guess he was beat, too.

I picked up my Kidzgo, the mostest, bestest, absolutely coolest gaming device EVER! RIGHT? I started to punch in a few commands, but then I yawned ridiculously big. Heard my jaw pop! And…last thing I remember is the Kidzgo falling onto my stomach. In a dreamy state and from somewhere very far away, I thought I heard the radio. *Did Grandma turn on the news?*

Boy Faces Arctic Storm To Save Local Family

Local news stations have learned that a fifth grade boy, wearing only flannel superhero pajamas, braved the recent record-breaking blizzard cold to save a family stuck in a drafty outbuilding. He fought his way through 100 yards of blinding snow to wrap up the parents and little ones and carry them to safety.

The boy said he had been tracking a big cat that may have been stalking local herds when he found the helpless family. The young hero said, "I stalked my prey and saved the day with only a rope and a toy." His story and words have been picked up by national news, and he will be interviewed on the Early Morning Journal on TV station K-I-D-Z-G-O next week.

The boy's school held a celebration

and invited the town to the civic center where they served Switzerland's world-famous thick dark hot cocoa drink in casserole bowls with floating marshmallows as big as baseballs. Everyone attending received a free tracking game piece.

Never, ever has a boy been excused from fifth grade state tests by becoming a local hero! Never, ever has there been such a successful adventure for any boy in the history of the world...

...or so Sam dreamed.

Glossary and Story Questions

Squatters people (or in this story, cats) who occupy an outbuilding (uninhabited and unlawfully) or on unused land.

Chartreux This beautiful but rare breed of cat has a fascinating history in France and recent popularity in the United States. Here are a few particulars about "Big Cat," the Chartreux:

- large and muscular body (called 'cobby') with short limbs
- orange/copper-colored eyes
- blue-grey or charcoal blue thick, plush (double coat) fur
- prized mousers (hunters)
- a seeming smile due to the shape of their heads and tapered muzzles
- silent (little meowing) but very vocal (clicks, chatters, throat noises)

Do **you** have a pet? How would you **describe your pet(s)** with bullet points as above?

Mosey means to walk or move in a leisurely manner. The next time your friend asks you to do something, say, "Sure! I'll just mosey on over there and take care of that for you!" Write your friend's response.

Ill-Bred This is a critical characterization of someone who may have been born to a poor, ignorant, unproductive, and perhaps criminal family. In this case, Sam was saying that Big Cat was arrogant of his status as the prized house cat and that the barn cats that ran in the wild were not welcome in his upscale world.

Cheshire Nose In this story this phrase is simply comparing Big Cat's arrogant (nose in the air) with a famous cat. But did you know that the Cheshire Cat is fictitious? The Cheshire Cat was made popular by the *Alice in Wonderland* stories and movies. Wikipedia has a very interesting entry about this cat. Read all about it and draw one.

Drink of Kings Hot cocoa or hot chocolate has been around for about 1500 years and is now enjoyed in many different ways around the world. Before the 17th century the Spanish court of King Charles V adopted the drink, and it became popular among wealthy people. It was very expensive. Cocoa was even given as a dowry (wedding payment) when the Spanish Royal Family married other European aristocrats. Perhaps, if Sam knew a little cocoa history, he associates this drink with kings. What do you think?

Marking His Territory Not only tomcats (males) but also female cats may mark the territory they consider their own. Perhaps you have seen a cat who backs up to a wall or shrub or grass patch, lifts the tail high in the air, and sprays the surface with urine, tail quivering? If so, you have seen a cat marking its territory. Cats may also "mark" an outdoor spot to indicate they are ready to breed. This marking may also send a message to other cats about their status on the property. Indoor cats usually use a clean litter box you have provided for them, but occasionally they "spray" a various places indoors as well. The smell is quite offensive, and there are books and websites that offer information about curbing such behavior.

Carhartt Carhartt is a well-known and trusted brand name of men's durable coverall clothing, available as jeans, pants, bibs, jackets, etc. The clothing is often made of duck cotton and is water repellent. The better bibs have chest cover attached to the waist of pants and with shoulder straps. A few details of the bibs include numerous utility pockets, a hammer loop band, and double-front knee pads built in. An interesting advertising notice on a Carhartt website says, *"Incorporating the suggestions of railroad engineers, Hamilton Carhartt began making his first overalls in 1889. While we've added a few new technologies since then, our goals have remained the same for over 125 years: listen to the customers and give the hardworking men the best product out there. Our classic men's overalls and bibs offer protection from the bottom of your beard to the heels of your feet. (Check out our boots for protection to the tips of your toes). Our overalls are available in various styles and sizes including denim overalls and big and tall bibs. Whether you need unlined bibs to keep cool or insulated overalls to fight the winter cold, Carhartt's got you covered. Literally. Featuring new technologies such as FastDry® and 37.5®, our bibs and coveralls for men will keep your temperature on track, and comfort at an all-time high. After all, what's more comfortable and functional than a good pair of overalls? At Carhartt, we believe these bibs are the birthright of all hardworking American men, especially when working in the dirt and mud is a family tradition."*

If you were going on an adventure that included harsh outdoors conditions including cold, wet, and/or snow, **name the pieces of clothing** that you have at home right now that you would wear.

Black Wrought Iron Fence Post is a type of
iron as opposed to cast iron; this iron is said to be "wrought."
It is tough but soft enough to shape. This iron used to
make fences and furniture is usually gently twisted to make
beautiful grillwork.

Rope Path Have you ever followed a rope path? **Design
and describe one** in your own backyard. Invite a friend
follow to it.

There are numerous references to **"light" and its
opposite**, "dark, dim, gray, etc." in this story. There are at
least a couple dozen lines that contain such references. Can
you find them all?

What is the **last real thing** Sam did?

Small Brown

for Quinci

Banished to the porch swing after breakfast for yet another argument with Mom, Katja[†] wiped a trickle of frustration from her eyes to her skirt. Jonah grabbed his four-inch beech tree twigs and glue bottle to head to the side porch. He could build his rustic log cabin without his sniffling sister.

The sun was warming the porch now. Katja heard dry leaves rustle and a thump behind the oak in the yard. She stood silently and moved to the open edge of the wooden porch. She lay on her tummy with her head hanging off the edge. Her view was rewarded. That fat brown bunny found the patch of fresh grass again. There were young yellowish green starts of the season, sprouting from the tangled moss and a few leftover winter leaves at the base of the oak. The rabbit had returned every day for a week. Katja knew because, it seemed, she ended up on the porch swing in time-out every morning.

The rabbit wiggled her hindquarters grandly, then plopped down to begin chewing. Her great bright white tail was the size of a door knob, quite large for a small brown wild rabbit. At her usual hunkered-down spot by the tree, her hind caught the morning sun and the cottontail seemed to glow. Another odd spot on the rounded back of the rabbit's neck was a shape like lips. It was bright white, too, without a single brown hair. It looked like the sun had kissed the little bunny's neck.

"So what do you argue about with *your* mother?" Katja asked with a laugh in her voice. The rabbit looked up with eyes only. She didn't stop her tiny, busy mouth from nibbling to give Katja an answer. "I suppose you always do your kitchen chores exactly the way your mom says to do them, huh? What's wrong with sweeping the floor first, THEN washing the table? Why is it better the other way around? At 13, I think I can figure out how to clean the kitchen!" The rabbit turned her back to Katja, and one tiny foot scratched the belly so fast, the foot seemed a blur. Katja giggled and wished she could scoop up the little bunny in her own hands, tickling the buff belly herself.

How lovely it would be to have a pet of my own…like Small Brown, Katja imagined. And then a promise to the rabbit:

"I'd sit right here every morning and let you nibble grass from my apron while I smooth down your soft ears. I could read you some stories…" and then with sudden force,

Katja complained, "and that's another thing: the literature assignment isn't due 'til Friday. Why, that's four days away! I know I can read and answer all those questions within four days. Why do I have to have it done by TOMORROW?" Katja complained loudly.

"...because tomorrow is my day to host our Home Schooler's† Middle Group and literature is my specialty," Mom answered through the window. "My kids **will** be caught up and ready to participate **this** week!"

Jonah was walking through the kitchen and spouted, "She wasn't talking to you, Mom. She's confiding in her rabbit."

"Jonah Norland! Get out of my conversation!" Katja yelled from the porch.

"Get out of my life," the ten-year-old returned.

Small Brown fled. Mom directed Jonah to begin his morning chores and ordered Katja inside for another start on the literature assignment.

Mom instructed Katja to complete the lit assignment before lunch. The assignment read, "Read aloud *The Velveteen Rabbit* to a child under the age of ten." *Jonah's close enough!* Katja thought and then stretched out on the couch to finish reading the directions, "Discuss with the child which stuffed animals he or she owns, which is a favorite, and which he or she wishes would become real."

"Well, no thanks," Katja said aloud and punched her sofa pillow for a more comfortable dent for her head.

"No thanks what?" Jonah asked, sitting in his blue-and-gold sports beanbag chair in the living room corner. He was working on his own literature homework which was quite different from Katja's assignment.

"I'm not reading to you and I'm not discussing pets with you," Katja explained.

"What are you jabbering about?" Jonah asked, more interested in challenging his sister to a distracting discussion than caring at all what Katja meant.

"OK, I'm game!" And Katja sat up on the couch to look at her brother and read, "Which of your stuffed animals would you like to become pets, Jonah? Which ones do you wish were real?" Katja, too, was ready, after only fifteen minutes of schoolwork, for a distraction.

"Oh! Cool! I'd have an iguana, a tarantula, and a baby panda."

"Awwww! A real live baby panda? Cute-Ness!" Katja's voice oozed as she made tiny claps with her hands.

"No, the spider would be the real pet…" and here Jonah paused for dramatic effect, "…so he would climb all over the stuffed panda. Get it? Black creepy-crawly on black-and-white panda fur?"

"Eeeewwwww, gross. You're done, Son!" Katja exclaimed, throwing the sofa pillow at her brother. But Jonah began laughing his little boy laugh—hearty, knee-slapping, endearing.

"Just kiddin', Kat. Your turn. Which animal would you like to have for a pet? …like in the *Velveteen Rabbit* story?"

"Exactly! A little brown rabbit is exactly what I want!" Katja got excited thinking about a live pet of her own.

"Like the little thumper you talk to every morning?"

"Yes…like her!" Katja agreed dreamily and fell back on the couch to consider how Small Brown could become her own pet.

Jonah left the room to begin making sandwiches for lunch. As he cut the loaf of warm bread and clinked the knife, scraping the peanut butter jar, Katja imagined the CHINK sound of Dad's small rodent traps catching squirrel and skunk.

"No, no, no, no, too dangerous," she whimpered, imagining a smashed, broken Small Brown. Katja tapped her forefinger on her lips and scrunched her forehead, sober as a sage,[†] *Hmmmmm… The old rabbit-trap trick perhaps? An upside-down cardboard box raised on a stick with a carrot inside?* "Maybe," she whispered. *Let's see…she's always sitting right there by the oak…hey, what about a butterfly net? Maybe… I bet I'm faster than she is! Could this really work?* "Yes!" Katja squealed aloud.

"What?" Jonah asked from the kitchen, "Yes, what?"

"None of your beeswax!"[†] Katja answered, "And, I want Mom's latest raspberry jam on my sandwich, not grape jelly."

"Git yer own!" Jonah slurred. But Katja didn't care. With a big smile and a clap of her hands, Katja had decided and could nearly feel the warm, soft bunny in her arms. *First thing tomorrow morning…*

Katja stood from the couch making big plans for dawn. She imagined: barely morning, standing completely stiff and silent beside the oak, holding the butterfly net above her head and ready to… Katja held the imaginary butterfly net in the air and was just in the downswing when—

"Katja, did you read your assignment yet?" Mom interrupted her daughter's reverie.[†]

"Uhh, yeah, uhh, yes, ma'am. Hey, Mom…" Katja began skipping to the kitchen, "Can I get a pet?"

"What? Where did that question come from?" Mom asked, helping Jonah finish lunch details.

"Well...Mother! I am reading *The Velveteen Rabbit* by Margery Williams, as...you...know," Katja emphasized "as you know," to impress her mom with her firm focus on the literature assignment, "...and I realized, I'd be a great Rabbit Mama."

"Oh! Rabbit Mama, huh?" Mom laughed. "Let's eat lunch and discuss it later."

After lunch, the family worked in the gardens and played several outdoor games with other homeschoolers in the neighborhood. Small Brown took a back seat in Katja's mind during the busy afternoon.

Around 6 p.m. Dad started the grill and the family made supper together. Katja decided she should catch Small Brown before talking to the family about keeping her. And so, from the supper blessing until nighttime prayers, Katja thought only about having a rabbit of her own. That night, she slept in her day dress with the butterfly net gripped in her hand. Her alarm was set for 5 a.m. She had a date with dawn!

❧❧❧

"Get up, Monarch Girl!" Jonah shouted into her room. Katja awoke, groggy, the covers flung back and the butterfly net lay on her pillow like a crown on her head.

"Huh? Ohhh, what? Nooo! Pooo!" Katja sat up and slammed both hands on her bed. She realized she had hit the snooze button too many times. And... she didn't appreciate Jonah's jab about the butterfly net.

At breakfast, Katja tried to introduce her idea for catching Small Brown. But Mom halted the conversation with, "Honey, you cannot catch or keep a wild animal. He will die."

"She."

"What?" Mom was distracted but stopped suddenly and looked straight at Katja.

"She. Small Brown is a she, not a he."

"How. Do. You. Kno…?" Mom shook her head. "Katja, I cannot discuss this now. There are 17 homeschool students on their way here in one single hour for our literature lesson. Are you ready?"

The Norland Home School day was *maybe the best ever*, Katja thought, since all the students talked eagerly about their favorite pets or wannabe pets. Some discussed their stuffed animals and which ones they'd love to come to life: a unicorn, a Beanie Babies tiger, a penguin from the aquarium field trip. Katja enjoyed the chatter but couldn't help looking out the window frequently. She noticed that Small Brown stayed and stayed and stayed, nibbling in her niche in the raised oak roots, despite the noise of all the homeschoolers. Small Brown seemed fearless. Katja thought she could probably walk right outside and pick the bunny up in her arms. *Wouldn't that be awesome?* she thought, hugging her arms across her chest.

"…so I have to give away my Holland Lop-Ear[†] before we move," Sula Andersen pouted.

"Mrs. Norland, what's a Lop-Ear?" asked Jon Young.
"Well, Jon," Mom answered, "…since we are talking about Sula's rabbit, why don't you ask her directly?"

"A Holland is a dwarf rabbit—a very little rabbit even when full-grown. And lop-eared means the ears hang down beside the rabbit's head rather than straight up on top," Sula explained. The word "rabbit" struck Katja's consciousness and she tuned in to the conversation.

At snack time Katja thoroughly interrogated Sula about her pet rabbit. After the school day, Mom seemed to be in a good mood. "Wasn't that an interesting literature lesson, Kids?" she asked while cleaning up after 17 middle schoolers. "And so many of the students had compliments for me on the lesson today. What a splendid school day!"

Katja recognized "the hot iron" and decided to strike,[†] "Soooo, Mom. Do you think we could help Sula out by taking in her rabbit for just a little while…when she has to move? Lollipop is the Lop-Ear's name. Is that cute or what, Mother?" Katja waxed syrupy.[†] "Anyway, Sula was so sad today…" Katja showed a pouty-lipped sad face, "…Did you notice? And I'd love to help her feel better, wouldn't you, Mom?"

Mom ate it up and beamed. She looked proudly at her early teen daughter. "Well, honey, that is so thoughtful of you. Let's talk to Dad tonight." Katja suddenly felt hopeful that *The Velveteen Rabbit* story might come true for her!

After dinner, the Norland family discussed every angle, it seemed, about rabbit-keeping with a number of concerns about how it would fit their family lifestyle. Especially, they tried to convince her that wild rabbits could simply not be domesticated. But one thing they all agreed upon: It was high time for Katja to have some personal responsibility in caring for something other than herself. The word "selfish" was not spoken aloud, but even Katja conceded that she spends every possible moment thinking about herself rather than others—a very unpopular vice in her family and among the homeschooling community. Katja herself even bragged that she was sure that her mood toward her mom would improve immeasurably if she had a pet rabbit. Mom turned her face away to grin. In the end, Dad said they'd delay their decision until Katja had time to do some research about rabbit-keeping.

Katja's assignment suggested by her parents included internet searches and talking to other families that raised rabbits. So, for the next five mornings, Katja sat on the porch swing, not in time-out, but rather glued to her laptop. She searched images and characteristics of hundreds of different rabbits. She loved each one.

She watched videos of rabbit care posted by professional rabbit breeders and from county fair shows, from a pet shop's instructional "Go-Home" program and brief posts from families all over the United States. Katja found even an Australian post by a little boy who raised a Flemish Giant rabbit, 19 pounds, who wrote, "Kibbies, our rabbit, is more like the family dog than a rabbit!" Finally, Katja called several families in the area that raised a rabbit or bred rabbits for showing in competitions. She was able to visit four local families and actually help with their rabbit care.

After a couple weeks, Dad admitted he was very impressed by and proud of Katja's hard work on the rabbit research. However, Mom complained that a few of Katja's school assignments were hurried or missing altogether. The parents agreed that having a pet may be a good addition to the family, but doing well in school would always be their children's first priority. The Norland family agreed to shelter Sula's Holland Lop-Ear for awhile until one of the families found a suitable, permanent home for Lollipop. This would benefit the Norland family, giving them a chance to assess their daughter's ability to juggle three important tasks all at once:

(1) To give loving care to a dependent, living creature

(2) To master all schoolwork

(3) To participate in daily family life with a respectful attitude

The evening Sula's Lop-Ear was to arrive, Katja sat alone on the porch, trembling in excitement. She was completely confident her family would see that she could juggle all three expectations with flying colors. AND, she was sure that Sula's Lop-Ear would fit into her family perfectly and soon become her very own pet. Even so, she had the names and phone numbers of a half-dozen local people who were selling rabbits. And, her savings account would accommodate any of the rabbits' selling prices.

Katja looked east and west on her road hoping to see the Andersens' headlights. *Where are they?* She wondered. Suddenly, Katja heard a most faint hissing sound among the dry, crackly leaves. She was suddenly afraid that a snake might be winding its way around the porch. She stood up, but froze in place instinctively. She squinted toward the edges of the porch, but something further out in the yard caught her eye. Something white and wiggling close to the oak roots. It was dusk and very hard to see, but Katja recognized the twisted figure of her Small Brown buddy. The rabbit was standing on her hindquarters with her white belly exposed. Her whole body was quivering. The creamy pink inside her tall ears reflected in the porch light like two Hawaiian Punch Popsicles. Small Brown's head was bent with the two bigger front teeth nibbling at her own belly. Katja could see that the rabbit was sucking air between her teeth as she bit a chunk of fur from her belly and stuffed it into one cheek with tiny paws. She pulled at another chunk with her teeth hissing, and then stuffed that into her other cheek. Small Brown continued this process until her cheeks were as puffy as a chipmunk's, though her belly looked unharmed. Then, the bunny scampered away toward the neighbor's horse farm. Katja wondered at Small Brown's strange behavior and began to follow through the yard, but then saw headlights rounding the road! *The Andersen's...finally!*

Sula's dwarf named Lollipop was settled into a hutch on the covered back porch at Katja's house. Every day Katja fed, watered, and played with the little black rabbit...all black, that is, except one hanging orange ear. The bunny looked like a Halloween disguise. It was soft and warm, but the fur was a bit more prickly than Katja had expected. She had met and petted numerous rabbits in her research, and many were softer than Lollipop. Katja especially loved the fur on the Angora rabbits which had the most fine, wavy, and wispy fur of all. She loved to gently blow across the backs and heads of these rabbits and watch the fur part and fly away from her breath. "Petting Angora rabbits was like petting air," Katja had told Jonah. But petting Lollipop was like touching Dad's prickly new-beard face.

Katja had kept up with most of her homeschool assignments, but only because she decided to get up one hour earlier than usual each day. She didn't want to blow her chance to have a pet of her own, and she knew she needed the extra time for school work. Katja enjoyed sitting on the front porch, her books strewn around her. She also loved to see the front yard wake up to the sun. There was a great variety of birds that peeped, squawked, and zipped their way past the porch to the neighbors' bird feeders. She watched the huge horses pound their way around the fence at the farm across the road each morning. And, she continued to see Small Brown come to and go from the old oak roots. It seemed to Katja that Small Brown was thinner than a few weeks ago. She didn't notice any more fur-pulling exercises, but Small Brown was definitely nibbling more grass and further out around the tree than ever before.

This morning, Small Brown was running in circles around the oak. Katja had never seen this behavior before. Small Brown ran around the tree once, then stopped to stare right at the porch. She ran around the tree again, then made a giant hop toward the porch, back to the circle and around the tree again. This time Small Brown made a most silly-looking hop straight up into the air about three inches off the ground! Katja laughed out loud. The rabbit repeated this odd dance a few more times, and Katja couldn't stop staring.

Then, Small Brown jumped closer to the porch than Katja had ever seen her. The rabbit ran in a tiny, tight circle and continuously lifted her eyes to Katja. The rabbit stopped suddenly, out in the open yard, far away from the protection of the oak roots and only a couple steps from the porch. Katja waited, not breathing, for the rabbit to scurry away or return to her silly circles. But Small Brown stayed. She hopped hesitantly toward the porch. Then…more like a bunny walk—front paws first followed by back paws, a full bunny body length closer to the porch. Her eyes were fixed on Katja's face. One rabbit step closer, tiny beads for eyes were pinned on Katja.

A sudden dread came over Katja; she felt certain the rabbit was actually trying to communicate with her. She felt very weird, worried, and wondrous all at once. Of course, Katja had talked often to Small Brown, but the rabbit had always seemed uninterested and certainly never communicated back. Could the rabbit really be trying now to tell Katja something? The girl stood; a textbook fell to the porch floor, but the rabbit didn't run away. Katja took a gentle step toward the front of the porch, but still the rabbit stayed. Small Brown was panting little hissing breaths, eyes fixed, hunched and trembling violently, but the rabbit stayed.

Katja looked behind her into the house. Mom was juggling the coffee pot, and Jonah was yawning and stretching his way down the hall. As she turned her head back to Small Brown, the rabbit was stepping away. A step and a hop and a turn of her little brown head to look at Katja, another step, a hop, a turn for a look. Step-hop-turn-look, step-hop-turn-look. Surely, the rabbit was beckoning Katja to follow, or so she felt. And, so she did.

Katja followed Small Brown to the end of her front yard, across the country road, through the ditch leading to the horse farm fence. The rabbit slipped under the fence, but Katja knew it was electrified. She couldn't touch it and the cross wires were too close for her to slip her pre-teen body through the fence. When Small Brown turned to look at her face, Katja mouthed, "I can't." The rabbit turned now, not only her little head, but also her entire body to face Katja. She thumped her hind leg on the ground once, twice, ten quick tiny thumps, and all Katja could do was stare. *Is Small Brown demanding I follow?* Katja was agog.[†]

"Kat! Breakfast, Kat!" The girl heard her name faintly, shook her head to clear her thoughts, and turned automatically toward her house. Jonah was yelling at one side of the porch, then at the other side. Without looking back over her shoulder at Small Brown, Katja ran like the wind toward her yard. She felt more afraid of the unnatural communication she left behind than any concern for answering Jonah's call.

"What were you doing over there?" Jonah yelled as she leapt onto the porch.

"None of your business," Katja retorted with a flushed face. She rushed past him and toward her own room.

After breakfast, while grooming Lollipop and then throughout the entire school morning, Katja felt a buzz in her head, heat in her armpits, and a rolling in her stomach. She spoke little to anyone. She told Mom she needed a nap after lunch. Although her mind was still racing, Katja fell into a hard, dark, dreamless sleep. Two hours later, the girl awoke but not refreshed. She took a bowl of ice cream and a math notebook to the porch swing.

There in the yard, Small Brown was waiting for her. In a fright, Katja dropped the bowl and the rabbit hid behind the oak. "You scared me!" she cried, automatically blaming the rabbit. She sprayed the dumped ice cream off the porch with the garden hose. She took her math assignment inside. *I have to find out if I am crazy or if I should be helping this rabbit.* Katja finally decided to stop the endless cycle of thoughts in her head. She stepped through the front door onto the porch. Small Brown was curled up at her usual nook at the oak roots, her pretty white tail sparkling in the sun. She was staring at the porch. Katja returned the rabbit's stare for a moment and then spoke to Small Brown, "I am going to visit my friend Lindy at the Horse Farm. You may join me, if you wish." The rabbit sat up tall.

Then Katja shouted into the house, "Mom, I'm going to see Lindy for a bit of science help." The girl secretly hoped her strong, fearless voice would scare away the rabbit. Katja even stamped her foot and yelled into the house as loudly as she could, "OK! So, I'm leaving now!" But Small Brown just stared.

Katja walked stiffly down the first step facing forward, but watching the rabbit out of her peripheral vision.[†] No movement from the rabbit. Small Brown seemed frozen. Down the next step, again with a sideways glance at the rabbit. Still no movement. Down to the third and final step and then, into the yard. Now the rabbit moved…but not away from Katja; rather, she made one big hop toward the girl. Katja moved on through the yard toward the road and, sure enough, the rabbit followed. When she got to Lindy's front door, Small Brown hid behind an ornamental grass patch. Katja rang the doorbell.

"Katja, hey!" Lindy answered the door with her science text in hand.

"Hey back to ya. You got time for a little experiment?"

"Sure! I just happen to be working on our science assignment right now." Lindy grinned, holding out her text.

"Not the science in that book, Lindy. The science… or mystery of animal communication," Katja said with her eyebrows raised. Lindy broke into a huge smile. Lindy believed in all sorts of mysteries of nature,[†] especially having to do with animals. Since she grew up in a horse family, she knew a lot about animal behavior and interactions. She would love to discuss Katja's queries.

After Katja told Lindy the whole story about Small Brown, Lindy peeked over her friend's shoulder and saw the little hunched rabbit's tail twitching and glowing in the sun. "Let's go," she said. The girls nonchalantly[†] walked into Lindy's front yard and toward the stable gate. Small Brown followed afar off. Lindy opened the great doors to the stable, and the rabbit raced ahead of them to the fourth stall. Small Brown ducked under the stall gate and disappeared. The girls suspected the rabbit had a nest, but neither could guess why Small Brown would bring them along to her home. They kicked around the bedding straw to try to find a little rabbit hole. Then Lindy mucked[†] a bit while Katja peeked under tack boxes, saddle racks, and feed bins. Neither girl found a tell-tale hole nor even any rabbit droppings. But after a bit, in a two-inch crack in the corner of Stall Number Four, Katja noticed torn rabbit fur. "I bet this is it! Come here, Lindy. Do you really think Small Brown led us here? Why would she want us to know about her home?"

"I don't know? Babies?"

"Oooooooo! Babies? Yeah, I bet that's it!" Katja was completely enthralled.

"Well, Kat, if your little garden bunny lives down there, there's no way we can get her out. She's on her own. I'm surprised she gets in and out at all. My mare, Charity, sleeps right there and since she is about to foal,[†] she's been laying there a lot. We forced her outside for fresh air just this morning. Oh, Katja, I hope we are wrong. I hope there's not babies…"

Katja had already kneeled down to try to see into the crack. The smell was strong animal urine, but she could see wiggling furry bodies almost like caterpillars. And, Katja recognized Small Brown's beady eyes. Down deep in the crack, those eyes looked like they were pleading. "Yep, Lindy, I see babies! Isn't it wonderful?"

"No! No, it's not wonderful, Katja!" Lindy's voice trailed off, and her face turned red as she heard the stable groom whistle for Charity.

"What, Lindy? What is it?"

Lindy knew they had only a short time to try to rescue the rabbit family. She explained the groom would soon brush and water Charity. Then, he'd check the mare for birthing time...and that could actually begin active labor. Charity would go to her favorite spot...right there in Stall Number Four and trample the area. "Finally, she'll lie down with her rump right over the rabbit nest. When she gives birth the area will be flooded with the horse's body fluids," Lindy explained to an unbelieving and horrified Katja. Lindy further explained that after the birth, the groom would wash and sanitize the area, flooding it again with chemicals and water. None of these procedures would be any good for baby rabbits trapped in a cement crack.

Katja's face color drained, not only because of the graphic explanation of Charity's birthing, but also because she imagined the fate of the baby bunnies. She shuddered and stuttered, "But we have to...what can we...how long... just go and tell..." She began to pace in a circle around the stall. Hot tears squeezed up through her choked throat and out her nose and eyes.

Lindy rubbed her back and said, "Let me talk to Ywen.‡"

Katja returned to the crack, dropped to her knees and began to beg Small Brown, "Come out. Bring your babies to me. We'll keep them safe at my house. Why did you put your babies in such an unsafe place? Hurry, Bunny! One-by-one, pull them up to me. I will hold them gently. All of you can ride home in my apron. We'll get another hutch and you can be friends with Lollipop…" Katja's flurry of words kept her from noticing her tears plopping on Small Brown's tiny forehead. But now she broke down and cried aloud. Small Brown receded more deeply into the crack.

"NAW! Again, naw, Young Miss! No good!" The loud man's booming voice sounded angry. "Chirty come first!" The Welsh groom named Ywen could not pronounce correctly "Charity," the mare's name. "Barn is my business. You father trust me. You go to house, Miss. Take your friend. Rabbits no important. Chirty important!"

Katja looked around for something heavy, something sharp. She found a horse's splintery tub brush. There was also an old metal stirrup cast aside. She picked them up— weapons to protect or tools to deliver? She tried them, one after the other to slam and bang against the edge of the crack. *Just another inch wide; my hand can scoop you guys out,* she thought. The girl heard a heavy clip-clop entering the other end of the stable, Stalls Numbers 16 and 18. She beat at the cement furiously, but only a few tiny pieces of chipped stone rolled away. She bent her head toward the crack and saw Small Brown briskly rubbing her little face with her forepaws. White dust covered her brown fur.

Katja felt a hand on her shoulder. Lindy said, "Let it go, Katja. This is nature's way. We cannot fix it. Let's go to the house and make some hot choc..."

"NO!" Katja roared. "These rabbits ARE important. Charity has this whole big barn...let her go..."

"Who this baby crying girl?" Ywen yelled. Charity stomped her great hoof. She let out a startled whinny ending in a long and loud snort. "You see? You upset Chirty! Get out of her stall!"

"Katja, let's go..." Lindy reached for Katja's hand.

What happened next swirled everyone in surprise. Charity, the giant mahogany Bay,[†] whinnied loudly and spread her long back legs to pee on the walkway. Ywen looked daggers at the girls, but softly soothed the horse, "Come, my pet. Your baby most important of all." Ywen slipped Charity into Stall Number Six. The mare gently sat, then rolled to her side. She groaned and began to heave. She snorted and kicked the side of the stall. She bellowed. Lindy ran out of the barn yelling for her dad. Katja cowered in the corner of Number Four. She covered her face and head with her apron and plugged her ears with her fingers.

Suddenly, she felt a nudge at her knee and jerked away fearing it was a tarantula or a barn rat or some other horse stall monster! When she jerked her apron away from her face, Small Brown was sitting atop the crack. In the Mama Bunny's mouth was one wiggly caterpillar-like baby bunny. All Katja could do was stare. Sounds began to fade away: Charity's moaning receded to suggest a hushed conversation far away on a porch swing; Ywen's maternal cooing became a bubbling stream; and Lindy's agitated calling for Mom or Dad sounded simply like a chirping bird. Katja watched her

little garden rabbit rescue each one of her five babies and plop them into the girl's lap. Katja felt she was hostage in a beautiful brown, fuzzy, silent world.

When the last baby was delivered from the crack, Small Brown jumped aboard. Katja couldn't help but bend her neck to kiss the white fur at the back of Small Brown's head —exactly at the spot shaped like lips. She gathered the edges of her apron around her burden, pulled them close to her heart and rose to walk home. Her feet automatically took her out the barn door, across the gravel driveway, through Lindy's front yard, and eastward down the country road to her own house. At one point, Katja may have heard a great whinny or a gruff voice, "Hey there!" She may have heard Lindy's voice; she may have heard her own name. But Katja couldn't be sure. She didn't see or remember a car whiz around her or the strong wind blowing twigs and debris along the ditch or the beginning rain drops. Katja walked as in a trance to her covered back porch.

Her family stared. Their eyes grew large and their mouths moved, but Katja couldn't really hear a thing; she couldn't respond. They touched her shoulder and patted her hair. Katja had eyes only for her burden. She offered a glazed look and a slight smile to her family, but she didn't speak. She filled a box with straw and lay her apron as a blanket for her soft little family. She set a bowl of water before Small Brown and pulled garden greens for the corner of the box. Dad set about building a large rabbit hutch, while Mom stirred up Katja's favorite cookies. Jonah stared at his sister as if she were a goddess.

For the rest of the day, Katja's head was swimming with snippets of scenes from the horse barn, the frantic hammering, the long walk home, the wriggling warm bundle against her chest. Katja's ears were dull as if filled with cotton. The phone rang all evening, but no one answered. Tomorrow they would talk. Tomorrow they would name one of the new babies, "Velveteen." Tomorrow Small Brown and Katja would sit on the porch swing together, grass spread in Katja's crisp white apron. She'd smooth down the rabbit's soft ears and read her stories.

Glossary and Story Questions

Katja Say *KAHT-yah*. This feminine name may have originated in ancient Greece, but today is related to dozens of similar names in as many languages, especially German, Russian, Dutch: Catherine, Kathleen, Katrina, Kathy, Katica, Caitlin, Ekaterina, Catalina, and over 100 other names! Katja means "pure, virginal." Do you know in what language your own name began and what it means?

Homeschool This popular term in North America is also known as home education, especially in Britain and Europe. The term refers to a family taking the responsibility to educate their own children in their home or in cooperation with other families. Such education is generally conducted by a parent, a tutor, or a degreed professional. Courses of study generally try to accomplish at least state or local education standards. Families or cooperatives (groups of homeschoolers) may use teaching materials as varied as the family's own written curriculum to highly organized and professionally printed Grades K-12 courses.

Homeschooling families often include school time for whole person development as compared to formal public education, i.e.,

- home management (chores, cooking, budgeting, etc.),
- relationship development (spiritual and emotional emphasis in relationships, as well as mental and cognitive camaraderie),
- time management and independent study activities,
- natural studies (Earth as our home, outdoor wonder and investigation, animal care, gardening, etc.)

Philosophies undergirding and initiating homeschooling generally include a family's wish to provide educational opportunities more in line with family values and with less interaction with public education. Many homeschooling families declare a preference for pursuing religious freedom in their education.

The U.S. National Household Education Surveys reported *National Totals of Homeschooling in the United States: 2012*, published November 2016 by the U.S. Department of Education: "...the homeschooling rate—has increased over time...from 850,000 students or 1.7 percent in 1999 to an estimated 1.8 million homeschooled students or 3.4 percent in 2012." The authors of the scholarly report are Jeremy Redford, Danielle Battle, and Stacey Bielick at the American Institutes for Research; Project Director, Sarah Grady.

And, "...as of March 2016 there are about 2.3 million homeschooled students in the United States," according to Brian D. Ray, Ph.D., president of National Home Education Research Institute (NHERI), *Research Facts on Homeschooling, General Facts, Statistics, and Trends.*

According to the research figures above, can you determine **what percentage** of students, nationally, were being homeschooled as of March 2016? Show your math ☺

Are you personally familiar with homeschooling? List two differences and two similarities between a homeschooler's education and formal public education.

Sober as a Sage A sage is a person who is very wise or known for wisdom, good judgment, and a long life of experience. Often such a person is known for his or her practice of studying and discussing large life questions or world/human situations. A sage may be characterized by sober and serious thinking.

Beeswax This term is informal slang in North America meaning, "none of your business!" Of course, the business of bees is to make a home, a honeycomb for their queen. Bees do this by secreting wax. This wax may also be harvested by humans and used to make wood polishes and candles. So... in a sense, the bees' business could become our business, too.

Reverie absent-minded daydreaming. When was the last time you daydreamed or was caught in a reverie?

Holland Lop-Ear is officially called The Holland Lop. It is an excitable little rabbit breed which originated in the Netherlands. The show quality of a true dwarf Holland Lop is 2-4 pounds. The ears are thick and short but hang vertically, but the rabbit has no control or ability to raise the ears up. Ears begin to lop from four to seven weeks of age. This is also the most critical time for the animal to be appropriately socialized for adulthood. The American Rabbit Breeding Association registry for this animal is the Holland Lop Rabbit Specialty Club (HLRSC).

Strike While the Iron Is Hot This is an old proverb...or idiom...or maxim or adage or truism or saying! These words describe short or trite expressions that quip generally accepted truth in common life experiences. Here's a Merriam Webster website to check out the differences and read about a few other sayings: http://www. learnersdictionary.com/qa/what-s-the-difference-between-idioms-and-proverbs

"Strike while the iron is hot" alludes to the hot forge of the blacksmith who must hammer out soft, melty iron while it is hot. If he waits for only a moment past the optimal time, the iron cools and hardens and his work piece fails. So, this saying could mean that it is best to do something quickly or immediately as soon as the opportunity is recognized rather than waiting and risk failing this one chance. Here's an essay on this very saying: http://www.writing.com/main/view_item/item_id/1173238-Strike-when-the-iron-is-hot-

Another similar saying is "make hay while the sun shines." Can you guess how this expression became a proverb?

Waxed Syrupy This is a take on the saying, "waxed philosophical." The saying means to wander in a conversation from the topic at hand or the facts of the conversation to invoking emotion or bigger life meanings suggested by the topic. Katja's conversation became overly sweet (syrupy) and pulled on emotion as she tried to convince her mother of her point.

Have you ever batted your eyes expressively, showed a fake pouty face, or especially, suggested that your idea will lead to great life goals such as world peace or ending hunger or saving the whales, etc.? If so, you may be learning to "wax philosophical."

Agog very eager or curious, amazed, and transfixed at some sight or sound. Perhaps related to the word "goggle," which indicates to look with widened or protruding eyes.

Peripheral Vision This is your vision on the either

side of your face, that is, what you can see on each side when your eyes are looking straight ahead. Often we notice only undetermined or indiscriminate movements or flickers on the sides without full vision, but good peripheral vision works well to alert us to things we should turn our heads to gaze at fully and possibly take averted action. Your parents may speak of good or poor peripheral vision for driving the car, "blind spots," etc.

Mysteries in Nature There is wondrous fascination with the powers of science and the scientific method. Sometimes there may be a dependence on science that ignores or disrespects the possibility for mystery. It is most interesting to note that there are many Earth mysteries that remain unsolved by science, there are places on Earth that have not been discovered or visited or explained, and there is animal behavior that cannot be completely defined. The two websites below may introduce you to Earth mysteries and recent scientifically solved mysteries:

- Mother Nature Network: http://www.mnn.com/earth-matters/wilderness-resources/photos/8-natural-mysteries-cant-be-explained/related-photos
- Care2.com: http://www.care2.com/causes/5-recently-solved-animal-mysteries-that-prove-we-know-nothing.html

Which animal mysteries might Lindy especially enjoy?

Nonchalantly means behaving and especially, walking, in a casual, calm, and relaxed manner, despite a tense moment. Example: walking with eyes forward, arms swinging, and perhaps whistling, so as not to indicate to anyone watching that you are really nervous, concerned, or afraid.

Mucked originally a British term, most people who keep horses knows well what this job is! It is to remove manure and other dirt from a horse's stable or other animal's dwelling. Informally, the word could mean to mishandle a job or a situation.

Foal as a noun is a young equine animal up to one year of age. Usually the term is reserved for a horse but may also describe a young donkey or mule. As a verb, foal means the pregnant equine gives birth. Wikipedia, dictionaries, and horse books will provide you with more information, but following I've listed a few of the many terms that may be associated with horses. Do you know each meaning?

Colt   Filly   Mare   Foaling   Suckling   Weanling
Yearling   Gelding   Stallion   Pony

Ywen Pronounced *EE-wen*, it is a variant of a masculine Welsh name Owain, anglicized to Owen. These are "given" names or "Christian" names as opposed to surnames, which is a last name. (However, Ywen may be a Chinese surname. There very few Ywen surnames in the United States!)

Owain (and its variants) has been a popular name in England for the last 100 years. It means "born of the yew (tree)." Yew trees may age to 600 years!! Just ten in England are believed to predate the 10th century! Besides it being a sturdy name (pun!), the name and the tree have special significance; see the article: https://www.woodlandtrust.org.uk/visiting-woods/trees-woods-and-wildlife/british-trees/native-trees/yew/

And especially this section from the article above, "Mythology and Symbolism - Yew trees have long been associated with churchyards and are abundant in southern England. There are at least 500 churchyards in England which contain yew trees older than the building itself. It is not clear why, but it has been suggested that yew trees were planted on the graves of plague victims to protect and purify the dead, but also that graveyards were inaccessible to cows, which would die if they ate the leaves. Yew trees were used as symbols of immortality, but also seen as omens of doom. For many centuries it was the custom for yew branches to be carried on Palm Sunday and at funerals. In Ireland it was said that the yew was 'the coffin of the vine', as wine barrels were made of yew staves."

We learn only a little about Ywen in this story, but from this bit of research above, and if such mythology surrounding our names should be true, could you "round out" Ywen's character and suggest any other activities or interests in Ywen's life? Have fun with this "character sketch!"

Bay is a hair coat color of horses, characterized by a deep shiny reddish-brown body color with a black mane, tail, ear tips and edges, and lower legs. These black areas are called the Bay's black points. Bay is one of the most common coat colors in many horse breeds.

Can you find the line early in the story that **foreshadows** the very last line?

Notice any **descriptive light words** or allusions to light. List them.

What **personal qualities** show up in Katja's adventure that may convince her family that she may be a good "Rabbit Mama."

Describe the five baby bunnies as you wish with **variations of markings** that suggest light (like their mama's sun-kissed spot on her neck). Of course, you may name them, too, if you wish! Remember, one is already named Velveteen!

Write an "added scene" anywhere in the story that suggests light—either a natural light, a mechanical light, or a psychological/spiritual light, i.e., new understanding or revelation.

What might have been happening to Katja when the world faded away in the last four paragraphs?

Transform and Roll Out

for Phynix

"**M**om, get them out of my room…Mom!" Bart stomped his foot and growled like a lion at his little twin sisters. Brinn ran out crying, but Betts stomped her foot back at Bart and stuck out her tongue. And then, she ran off, too. Twelve-year-old Bart sometimes acted like he was "man of the house." *God knows we need a man of the house around here!* He thought. But Bart desperately wanted Dad to come back home and be man of the house.

"You girls think my room is open season,[†]" Bart shouted down the hall. But this may have been his own fault when, a few months ago, Bart had invited the twins to come in to play with his Transformer Toys.[†] Dad was sick and the girls were restless, Bart remembered. "But sometimes! I told them, sometimes! But today is not one of those sometimes," Bart grumbled aloud. But he was only trying to convince himself that he had every right to scare the girls off.

At barely age four, the twins didn't understand or care about Bart's longing for privacy. Nor did they understand that Bart was quite busy today with three important things:

(1) preparing for the dreaded middle school vocabulary test

(2) packing for the four-day Labor Day weekend with Uncle Owen

(3) finishing his model pirate ship for Dad's birthday gift

He didn't have the luxury of time for the twins under his feet. Bart wondered how Dad would handle the situation.

Well, first things first, Bart thought…but he chose the last and best thing first. He pulled out the fittings for the wooden model, a "ship o' yore"[†] which, he was sure, would be the best gift he'd ever given Dad! Birthdays were always special at Bart's house, but celebrations had grown thin since his dad was in and out of the hospital this past year. And now, Dad was back in.

Bart found his glue syringe, gently nuzzled the nose of the syringe into the belfry ring,[†] and squeezed a drop onto the bell's curve. He pushed the bell onto the ring and held it without breathing. *Steady, steady, steady*, Bart chanted to himself, allowing the glue to dry.

"She's a beaut, this Ochre!"[†] Bart imagined his dad

saying when he would unwrap the gift. But Bart would not hear Dad's voice for himself. Dad's operation was yesterday, and Mom will go alone to take the gifts to Dad in the hospital.

Bart remembered when he was the only kid in the family. Dad loved building and collecting old wooden model ships. He told Bart once that he'd always wanted to be a pirate and, "...this is the closest I'll ever git, Me Matey. Arrrrrhhgg!" Dad shut one eye and pretended to be a pirate. Back then, it was funny. Now, Bart thought that pirate stuff sounded pretty silly. But he would give anything to hear his dad talk like a pirate again.

Bart had learned a lot about his dad's old wooden ship passion after working on this project for the last few weeks. After he successfully attached the ship's bell into the belfry, he pulled the clapper to make it ring. It was real brass and pealed a strong chime. Bart learned the ship's bell was considered to be the "voice of the ship." It was used to mark the beginning of the watches or to ring an alarm when necessary. The bell also gave audible warning signals for other sea vessels when fog rolled in. Bart thought, *My own dad is the ship's bell for this family! I miss his voice!*

Bart opened the fittings box and pulled out the barrels and binnacle[†] to glue to the ship...

"Pleeeeeeease," whined the girls in unison leaning into his open bedroom doorway. Bart sighed a long drawn-out, dramatic pre-teen sigh, sounding like a steam engine slowly pulling into the train station. "Mama say we aks nice, you let us play wiff Bumblebee. Soooooo, pleeeeeeease?"

"Hello, Girls, thanks for knocking," Bart sighed with an edge of sarcasm.

"We didn't knock." The twins looked at each other in complete surprise.

"Riiiiight!" agreed Bart. "Well, OK, c'mon in. Now, let me think. Nah, not Bumblebee. How 'bout I let you play with Jazz—he's the best of the Human Alliance against the Decepticons." The girls didn't look impressed. "Or, or how about Optimus Prime…ya know, we named him 'Opy?' He's a Classic AND a Voyager, Girls!!" Bart tried enthusiasm and persuasion in his voice. Still no smiles from the four-year-olds. "C'mon, Girls. Bumblebee is my Cyber Stompin' Dude, my only Transformer with lights and sounds. He likes it up on my shelf," Bart resisted.

"Jazz looks too mean; anyway, he's dead!" Betts was pretty blunt. Bart wished he had never told the girls the movie story of the Jazz Transformer, who died at the end. *Ah! Such is the danger of giving away the secrets of the Transformer Universe to g-i-r-l-s!* Bart slowly spelled out the last word in his mind while squeezing his eyes shut.

"Yeah," agreed Brinn…always agreeing with her twin, "And your ol' Opy has big guns. Mama says no to guns…but he is pretty," Brinn had found Opy on the floor next to the door and was already pulling out the blue legs and twisting the red arms of the autobot into place…and pointing the silver gun.

"Alright, Girls, but no Barbie clothes on my Bumblebee Transformer today," Bart grinned. Betts quickly hid her Barbie Bag behind her back and nodded, happy as a hyena. Bart knew the bag was full of skirts and hats for her dolls… and the Bumblebee Transformer! But he didn't disapprove. Brinn grabbed the bright yellow Robot in Disguise from the animated series and hugged him to her chest. She pressed the button on his big fist and it popped out. His eyes lit an azure blue and his chest lights flashed yellow and white beams. The girl was delighted and walked away in a daze.

Bart knew there was a burden in being "man of the house" for the girls and, at times, for Mom. He never told anyone, but he was plenty scared about Dad's sickness. *Those bad dreams*, Bart started thinking…

"Thanks, BoBo!" the girls squealed in unison.

"Bart, Girls. The name is Bart. I'm big now!"

"OK, BoBo, we-we-we mean, Baaarrrt!" They giggled together and ran down the hall.

"Must be nice to be so little and not know yet about the big scary stuff of life," Bart mumbled, thinking again of his dad.

∽∽∽

On Thursday morning before Labor Day, Bart asked Mom to help review his vocabulary words[†] at breakfast. He started, "Thread – a long piece of string or a conversation on the internet."

"Well, honey," Mom commented with a grin, "I don't know if you're supposed to remember every word in the definition, but yours is a bit 'thin.'" Bart didn't get the pun. "Thin, Bart, 'thread' means a long, THIN strand of fiber to make cloth or used to sew cloth together. Anything that is very thin…and, I suppose…just like a topic being discussed on the internet. Those threads certainly ARE thin!" Again, the pun escaped Bart, but Mom chuckled at her own wit.

"OK, OK…a long thin thing," Bart skipped over the correction. "Let's go on. Uhhh…Texture – something that feels bumpy," Bart remembered.

"Well, yes, the definition here is 'rough and raised,'" corrected Mom.

"That's bumpy, right? Next?"

"OK," Mom sighed. "Transform."

"Transform…" repeated Bart, "…is a toy that changes from a car or a ship to a robot…"

"Bart," Mom interrupted, "this is not a reference to your collection of toys called Transformers. The word here is 'transform.' Let me read the definition to you, 'Transform means to make a thorough or dramatic change in the form, appearance, or character of.' Transform, Bart, means to change from one form to another, like a caterpillar to a butterfly or how you are turning all those little wooden and metal pieces of your model into a pirate ship…or, or…" Mom was on a roll now. "…or like Dad's liver transforming from canc…" Mom stopped so suddenly that mother and son only stared at each other in silence. "I'm sorry, Bart, I didn't mean…" Mom looked away and wiped her face. "You'll do OK on your test today, honey."

During homeroom, Bart felt discouraged. The vocabulary test was just hours away and he wasn't sure he could define any of the words. And, worse, he worried about Mom. She never seemed to be happy anymore, for even a few minutes. *Yet, I know she is praying hard for Dad.* Bart took comfort in that, at least.

Bart looked out the classroom window during announcements and noticed a late bus arriving with flashing lights. He began to daydream about the azure blue blinking lights of his Bumblebee Transformer…something about those blue eyes; suddenly the eyes seemed to float all over the top of the bus. Then the bus became a large rolling casket. The casket lid began to rattle ajar. Bart gasped aloud, waking himself from his daydream to his classroom. Several students stared at him. He quickly opened a book and stole a glance back outside to the bus...whose door was creaking open for students' exit.

Fifth period hung like an axe over Bart's head all morning. The vocabulary test came and went just before lunch. In the cafeteria, Bart's friends were rehashing the test. "So... 'thread' and 'texture'... they're about the same thing, right?" guessed one boy, "...ya know, thread – material – texture – the feel of the material...it's all about cloth, right?"

"I don't know," grimaced another. "Too many 't' words; couldn't keep them straight. Isn't 'texture' and 'transform' the same thing?"

"No, no, no," Bart shook his head. " 'Transform' is the hardest one – has something to do with 'form,' like changing one thing to another...you know, like Transformer Toys?"

"Transformer Toys?!" asked one of the guys, an incredulous[†] look on his face, one eyebrow stretched up his forehead and his mouth gaping with a silly grin. "Like really, Man? You play with Transformers?"

Bart blushed but recovered, "Heck no! Those toys are for kids! But if you guys know what Transformers are, ya oughta know what 'transform' means!! Duh!" *Good Save, BoBo!* Bart congratulated himself.

Bart grabbed his lunch tray and headed to the sixth grade lunch table. "Anyway," Bart continued, trying to exude confidence to his friends. "I'm pretty sure I got most of the vocab words right." But he thought to himself, *I can only hope I scored at least half!*

Bart relaxed when the boys began debating another test, another teacher, the new girl at school, etc. Bart's mind raced ahead to his trip to Uncle Owen's after school. Uncle Owen is a homesteader in the neighboring state, a four-hour drive away. *He'll be at the house for supper, so I gotta finish packing as soon as I get home from school,* Bart thought, eating his lunch faster and faster, thinking that would make the day go faster. Bart was eager to explore the primitive land where Uncle Owen lived. He was excited, too, to help with chores, especially driving the tractor and herding animals. Bart thought about what Dad always said about his kid brother, "That Owen, the homesteader. He works day and night, building a good life outta nothin'!" Bart remembered how proud his dad was of Owen.

Anyway, Bart smiled and thought about how jealous his buddies would be. *Uncle Owen's homestead is like no other farm any of these kids ever saw! Talk about transformed! Wow!*

By 4:30 Bart had nearly finished packing when he began to debate which Transformer to stuff into his backpack: Jazz was a gift from Uncle Owen's own collection of Autobots and Megatrons. Bart wanted to impress his uncle that he had kept this one in such good condition. But then, the bright yellow Bumblebee was Dad's present to Bart for his twelfth birthday last year. That meant the world to Bart. He and Dad were intending to create a Universe Cabinet for all his Transformers…but then Dad got sick again. Bart found Bumblebee in the corner, dressed in a Barbie prom gown. His poor yellow Cyber Stomper's eyes were NOT flashing —*probably too embarrassed!* Bart thought, laughing aloud. But he stuffed Bumblebee, as is, into the backpack.

Giggles outside his door made Bart check the clock— had he run out of time? Was Uncle Owen here already?

"What, Girls?" Bart said over his shoulder toward the closed door. More giggles. "What do you want, Girls?" Bart's voice turned sour with irritation.

"Can we come in, BoBo, we have a kesjun," Brinn's laughter had turned to a pleading whine.

"You mean you have a 'ques--tion'?" Bart enunciated[†] the word slowly and emphatically. "What is your ques-tion?" Bart was still talking through the closed door as he reached for Jazz and Opy, weighing them in his hands. *Which one or both, which one or both?* he wondered.

"Well...uhmmm...can me see you face?" asked Betts.

"Why do you have to see my face to ask a quest...oh, for crying out loud..." Bart suddenly pulled his door open, startling the twins, who were leaning against the door. They tumbled in and rolled like puppies over Bart's big feet. All three began laughing. Seeing Bart happy, the girls grabbed each others' hands and danced in a circle.

"OK, Twinsies," Bart smiled, "what's the question? Brinn, say 'quesss--chunn.' " Bart emphasized both syllables.

"Kessss--jun," repeated Brinn quite studiously.

"Good 'nuff." Bart scratched the top of Brinn's curly hair.

"We...we..." and the giggles started again. Bart's face fell with instant impatience. Betts got serious, "We be Transformers at Uncle Owen's house?"

"You mean you want to play with MY Transformers all weekend?"

"Well, sometimes, if is OK wiff you, but..." garbled Brinn. Giggles again.

"Girls!" Bart wondered, what is it with these two? Either whining or ridiculous giggling! "I still have packing to do so..."

Betts spoke loudly and very, very fast, "Can we wear your old Transformer T-shirts for plaaaaaying...for sleeeeeping and...and...and..."

Brinn whispered, "Mama said we can aks you betause you got too big...you gots lots shirts too little for you."

"OK," agreed Bart. "I get it." In reality, he was proud that his tiny twin sisters loved Transformers as much as he did...still does! "Knock yourselves out, Twinsies. The clothes I've outgrown are in the basket in the closet. BUT CLEAN IT UP WHEN YOU ARE DONE! Ya hear me?"

"Yeth, BoBo," the girls said at once.

"Bart. My name is Bart," he mumbled looking at the ceiling.

သသသ

From the east side of Indiana to the west side of Illinois, Uncle Owen asked questions that kept the kids talking. They chatted about sixth grade and pre-school, friends and play groups, church and youth groups, and hometown sports. Bart often had to interpret some of the girls' ill-formed words for Uncle Owen.

But Uncle Owen didn't ask about Dad. Bart wanted to talk about Dad. He was already feeling lonely, maybe homesick, because he hadn't been able to talk to Dad for days. His mom couldn't talk about Dad without crying. And since the kids were staying with Uncle Owen for the next four days, Bart guessed Dad was serious enough that Mom was going to stay in the hospital with him.

Those awful dreams... Bart fretted as he looked out the window, dusk rushing by. His eyes glazed over and he began to daydream. The chatter in the car faded away, and Bart felt or imagined...or perhaps he really saw in the sky over the wavy rushing landscape a pair of eyes, those blue azure eyes, flashing eyes, watching him, fading away but then returning. Then...Bart saw the caskets again; many styles, colors, and sizes of caskets; clods of dirt flying all around, bouncing from one casket to another. The blue eyes far away, then closer, watching everything. Suddenly, as if in a whirlwind, the caskets were bouncing into each other and beginning to split apart. Bart shut his eyes and his hand came instinctively to his face. He didn't want to see what might be inside the caskets.

"Uh-Oh!" The girls were squealing with laughter.

"Just call me 'Uh-Oh!' " Uncle Owen was saying to the girls. " 'Uh-Oh!' for short."

"Wh-what?" Bart wondered aloud, allowing the conversation in the car to press into his dazed mind.

"Yeah, I was just trying to help the girls enunciate all the syllables in my title and name. Un-cle O-wen. Pretty imposing for four-year-olds, don't ya think, Bart?"

"What did you say was your nickname?"

"Uh-Oh."

"Why would you want us to call you something so dum....uhm, different?" Bart asked.

"All my buddies call me that! During the first couple seasons on this neglected land, the work was so overwhelming that all I could say all the time was, 'Uh-Oh!' " The twins liked that explanation and giggled.

So the girls began to repeat the nickname constantly with a jingle in their voices, "Uh-Oh, Oh No, You did a Boo-Boo! No, no, Uh-Oh, the doggie went doo-doo!" Bart rolled his eyes but Uh-Oh was eating it up with the girls, making more ridiculous rhymes moment by moment. Finally, Bart succumbed to the contagious laughter. The car was rollicking with pure happiness! And then one of the girls shouted, "Gotta pee, gotta pee." And she did.

The family exited the highway for a refreshment stop. Brinn didn't cry but was embarrassed by her wet clothes and car seat. Betts helped her sister freshen up and change clothes. The guys sprayed out the car seat and placed a soft blanket on the seat pad. They all tossed a little foam football around for 20 minutes and then had ice cream where the rhyming game started up again.

As they drove back the long lane of the homestead, even though it was nearly dark, Bart was agog at the changes to the farm he could see since he had visited three years ago. It had been a meadow land, sparse, with only a couple mature trees, but boasted a deep running stream and a large pond. Now, the lane was overshadowed by fifteen-foot trees with a heavy canopy[†] of every fall color. Bart had helped Dad and Uh-Oh plant starter trees and dig in posts for a grape arbor. Now the arbor was literally running through the trees, full of curly woody vines with leaves as big as Frisbees. The grapes were just ripening, some still a bug-green color and others pale purple. But each one big as a shooter marble.[†]

Fowl flocks scattered at the approaching car: a dozen plump chickens with feathers of every design and color, mostly shades of browns, reds, and grays. There were four squawking, scolding roosters. One jumped right up onto the hood of the slow-moving car and pecked the windshield. Ducks waddled away with their curly tails wiggling. But three giant turkeys with the bluest snood and wattle[†] Bart had ever seen refused to move out of the way. The fleshy skin around

the turkeys' heads and throats flapped as they gobbled more loudly than the sound of the car engine. Uh-Oh honked the horn and the turkeys began to dance away.

Bart saw on the horizon a large white barn and three red sheds behind the two-story cabin which was Uh-Oh's home. Fields of crops were laid out circling the house and fenced pastures herded a few cows, goats, and sheep. Instead of a front lawn, Uh-Oh had dug in gardens of vegetables, flowers, and herbs with a meandering straw path throughout. The gardens were book-ended by a gazebo on one side and a tall wooden crate holding compost on the other.

By the time they unpacked the car, Bart's eyes could not take on one more intriguing sight…and he could barely keep them open. The twins were already asleep.

By the second morning at the homestead, all of Bart's muscles were yelling at him. He had kept up with Uncle Owen on all the chores for two whole days; but now, he couldn't get out of bed. He heard that the twins were up, though. Their giggles and running footfalls zipped past his bedroom door a dozen times since daybreak.

Uncle Owen's girlfriend, Steph, had come by each day to play with the girls and teach them some basic homesteading. And now, she was trying to herd them to the breakfast table. Bart smelled cinnamon rolls and Uh-Oh's strong coffee.

Bart pulled his complaining body out of the soft bed and began to "stretch awake," like Uh-Oh had taught him,

"In a couple days, you'll probably be pretty sore, BoBo," he had warned.

"Bart, Uh-Oh, nobody calls me 'BoBo' anymore," Bart corrected the first day on site. The family had called Bart that awful baby name since…well, since Bart was a baby. For the last two years, Bart had had his fill of feeling like a baby and was ready to be a grown-up…or almost.

"Oh! OK, Big Guy," said Uh-Oh with a grin. "So here's a good stretchout for you. It's simple. Stand with feet shoulder-width apart. Reach as high as you can and wiggle fingers. Point arms straight out at the shoulders, east-to-west, and pretend like you are trying to grab the opposite ends of the Earth. Now, pull the ends of the Earth to your sides. Then, the old hands on hips and twist exercise: turn top half of your body as far as you can toward your back, both sides, slowly and gently. Finally, squat with a straight back for two whole minutes."

So, this morning Bart began the stretches, but gave up when the ends of the Earth refused to budge. He slowly dressed and gingerly tip-toed down the stairs with little grunts, "ooh, ouch, uhh, uhhhh..." and sucked air in through gritted teeth.

"Hey, Bart, Buddy, did those squats do you in?" Uh-Oh was smiling too big.

"Somethin' like that," Bart replied, not too friendly. As he carefully sat his aching body in the chair, Steph kissed him on top of the head and scolded Uh-Oh.

"Don't tease the hardest worker you've ever had on this farm!"

"True dat!" agreed Uh-Oh. And Bart's shoulders pushed back instinctively and he raised his head with a nod toward Uh-Oh meaning, "Ha! Take that."

In the middle of the long log table strewn among the dishes of breakfast food, Bart saw a dozen of Uh-Oh's Transformer collection and a couple of Bart's, all standing at the ready.[†] "Whaaa..." Bart started.

"I'm declaring today 'Transformer Day!' Thought we should take the morning off, Bart, and talk Decepticons and Human Alliances," Uh-Oh said, with a twinkle in his eye.

"Yeah, look at us!" The twins held hands and arched their backs, showing off Bart's hand-me-down Transformer T-shirts in honor of Transformer Day: Betts in a Grimlock Dinobot shirt—a grey hunchbacked dino with silver tail, yellow feet, and red eyes—it was the eyes that Betts loved. And Brinn dressed in Armada Tidal Wave, the big brute of the Decepticon army. She just liked the giant picture of the bot stretched across her whole chest...and she loved the colors. Odd yellowish-greens, red stripes, greys, blacks, pale browns, and Brinn's favorite color, purple. This guy boasts purple legs, purple knobs and dials on his chest, and his name emblazoned[†] across the shirt in bold purple letters. Of course, Brinn topped it all off with a big purple bow in her hair.

After a sweet and steaming breakfast, Bart flashed Cyber Stompin' Bumblebee's blue eyes at Steph as a thank you for the great meal. The Bumblebee played a gravelly theme song from the movie, but it sounded like an electronic tone grumbling its muffled tune up from the basement. However, Bumblebee's eyes and chest knobs flashed faithfully in rhythm to the song. Steph tried to look impressed, then said, "The twins and I are going to tie up the garden herbs this morning and then go berry-picking for our supper pie. So, Gentlemen, we will need the kitchen table by mid-afternoon."

"OK! Transform and roll out!" Uh-Oh shouted, uttering the Autobots' rallying cry. Bart jumped up and cleared the table of dishes and flatware,[†] ready to rumble!

After two hours of destroying every Decepticon in the universe and saving the Earth over and over again, a phone call startled the guys. Uh-Oh stood to go to the den to grab the landline,[†] "Hey, Bobo, clean the jelly off Galvatron, would ya?"

"Bart, the name is Bart," the boy reminded his uncle.

"Bart, Bart, Bart, Bart, Bart," Uh-Oh chanted as he marched out of the kitchen. Bart grinned and thought, I gotta call Mom today.

"Oh, Susan, I'm so sorry," Uh-Oh was whispering now.

Susan? Susan is my mom... wondered Bart. He could hear only parts of words, "...you OK?...a diagnosis? ...what can I do?..." Bart was stricken with fear and ran toward the den, but the phone call was over before Bart could get there.

"So, Buddy...your dad had another operation—an

emergency last night. It was pretty serious, Bart," Uh-Oh was calmly explaining, "…but, the doctors are cautiously expecting recovery from the removal of the diseased part of the liver." He paused to let his words sink in. Bart's face was white and his blue eyes unfocused. Uh-Oh went on to try to draw Bart into the conversation. "I know you've studied a bit about anatomy in school and you probably know that the liver can regenerate itself…"

Bart's face suddenly twisted and he became livid[†] and loud, "I know! Everybody knows about livers regenerating! Why do you think you have to teach me everything? I'm not stupid!" Bart's face exploded with rage and tears. He ran to the guest bedroom and slammed the door shut. He forgot he was supposed to behave like a guest. He forgot he was dearly loved by Uh-Oh. He forgot he was mothered and admired by Steph. He forgot every good thing his parents ever taught him. Bart only wanted to scream in fear, confusion, and anger. And scream he did, into the pillow on the guest bed.

$$\text{֍֍֍}$$

The knock on the door was so faint, Bart imagined his toenail was scraping the wooden footboard of the bed. He turned over and pulled the quilt over his head automatically —he wasn't at all awake. Another knock roused him and he mumbled, "Uhhh?" more to himself than in answer to the knock. He heard the doorknob turn and a few footfalls. He was dazed and incoherent.[†]

Suddenly, Bart smelled two conflicting scents that nearly made him gag: warm raspberries and a girlie perfume. He bolted upright holding his mouth. "Hey! Hungry? You've

had a very long nap, Buddy," Steph whispered, standing beside the bed. She was holding a tray with a giant glass of icy white milk and a piece of steaming pie.

Bart rubbed his face and hair to appear presentable, but felt a hairy, dry, and stinky mouth—a feeling that made him embarrassed in the presence of a lady. "Mmmmmmm," with grinning but tightly pursed lips is the best he could do. Steph put the tray on the bedside table and tweaked Bart's ear and gave him her pretty white smile.

"See ya later, Gator!" She winked and was gone.

Bart let out a very stinky sigh. His face felt like crumpled paper, his eyes were swollen and itchy, his pillow was snotty, "Dad, Mom," Bart whispered aloud and teared up again. *Recovery*, Bart remembered Uh-Oh had said. *Is it possible?*

The pie was seeping blood-red juices and a couple dripping berries. The ice cube in the milk clinked the sides of the glass as it melted. Bart was suddenly famished.

"There's the man!" Uh-Oh exclaimed as Bart stepped into the living room. The girls ran to hug Bart's waist and he grinned.

"Hey, Twinsies!" He hugged their little necks. He forgot how good they smelled after their evening baths. But they were squealing, both at once, and dancing in a circle around Bart. All he could make out were phrases.

"...Dada libver get better...Steph teacher on compoooter..." Bart's face was askance.[†]

"....OK, Brinn, Betts," called Steph from the kitchen, "...your turns to stir the lemonade!" And they ran away as happy to leave Bart as they were to see him. *Fickle women*, Bart grinned.

Uh-Oh was tickling the keyboard of his old PC. He pulled his index finger into the air and then plunked it onto the Enter button with a smack, "...annnnnd done!" He turned to look at Bart with victory on his face, "You are now an on-line student through your own hometown school services!"

"What? Why?" Bart started.

"So much to tell you, My Man! But first, will you help me with evening chores? I got behind and the cows are bawling."

"Well, OK, I guess, but I just showered."

"That's exactly how farm life is, Bart. Just as soon as you think you're ready to relax, something messy and dirty has to be done! In fact..." Uh-Oh was proud of himself for waxing philosophical[†] on occasion, "...that's the way it is with anything in life!!"

"Whatever." Bart wasn't trying to sound disrespectful, but his head was still quite unclear about the turn of events in his family.

Not only did the cows demand an evening milking, which Bart had learned to do fairly well, but also the pig on the spit[†] required a few turns. Bart and Uh-Oh sliced a bit of fatback[†] and let the juices run up their arms as they nibbled the sizzling roast pork. Uh-Oh had talked constantly throughout the chores about the family's plan to keep the kids on the homestead for possibly a few more weeks, "....the time it will probably take for your dad to recover in the hospital and then at a rehabilitation center. Your mom is returning, at least part time, to work, Bart."

"So...in four weeks, Dad is better and I'll go back to school, right?" Bart, like most kids in difficult situations, simply wanted to know how his own life would change and when it would get back to normal.

"Oh, no, Son! When you go home, Bart, you will indeed be the 'man of the house' for some time. Your dad will need perhaps months of therapy and partial bedrest, due to other complications besides the liver. He will be on strong medications that will keep him pretty sleepy. Susan will have to work for some time. In a nutshell, YOU will run the house for your family, Bart." Uh-Oh spoke with a jingle in his voice as if he couldn't hear the whole world falling down around Bart's ears.

სესეს

For an entire month now Bart had run the homestead,[†] inside the cabin and around the whole farm, *ALL BY MYSELF*, Bart thought and then modified his boast with the truth, *well, I've done a lot of it alone, anyway*. Steph had flown to the West Coast to complete a university grad program and Uncle Owen had various meetings and work details with other homesteaders across the state. Owen was in and out of the house throughout each day, but was home every evening.

As Bart's tolerance grew for waking early, toning muscles with hard, physical work and for answering the twins' hundreds of questions every day, he settled into a "typical homestead schedule."

Bart started the mornings with animal care and gathering eggs, herbs, and strawberries. He had learned how to make the most flavorful scrambled eggs with fresh thyme and oregano which he picked straight from the herb patch. Then he sprinkled the fresh strawberries with mint leaves and poured fresh cold goat's milk over the berries. This breakfast dessert was actually a breath freshener as well, so the three kids often skipped morning tooth brushing.

After breakfast, Bart showered and began his two hours of morning schoolwork online. As he left the kitchen, he always set up the morning for the girls, "Whose turn is it to check the locks today?"

"My turn," one of them squealed and they rarely argued over whose turn it really was. She flew like the wind to the three entrances of the cabin, securing locks. The house was always kept locked if Uh-Oh was away and Bart was busy with his schoolwork in the upstairs office.

The other twin knew it was her turn to put food from the table back into the refrigerator or cupboard, so she would run in the opposite direction. "Now check the face clock, Girls," Bart instructed and they recited where the long hand and the short hand should be when Bart would be back downstairs.

Steph had taught the girls how to clear the table and make a sink of warm soapy water to soak the dishes until lunch. The girls also had dolls and the Transformers to play with. Steph had started them on a project to make the biggest yarn ball ever. She wrapped strips of cloth around a tiny one-inch rubber ball and showed the girls how to rip more strips into thin pieces and carefully wrap them around the ball. They loved choosing an old shirt or skirt or towel from the craft box and tearing the strips, then wrapping the ball. They easily spent an hour or so before they got bored. So far, the ball was a five-inch diameter.

Bart had learned some handcrafts as well. He made his first-ever wood project—a step-stool—for the girls to wash and rinse dishes together. Uh-Oh created the design and supervised, but Bart did all the board ripping[†] and nailing. The twins were thrilled with their little bench and practiced kitchen-cleaning often. Whenever Uh-Oh was in the room, he always made a very big deal over their busy little hands and feet. They loved pleasing Uh-Oh so they learned quickly where everything belonged in the kitchen and how to clean up after a meal. Of course, they usually wiped the table with a too-wet sponge, but no one corrected them. "Water dries," someone would always say.

The twins also loved to use their little wooden corn brooms to sweep the floors. Bart and Uh-Oh had cut down and sanded small brooms for the girls' heights. They often voluntarily took their brooms to sweep the wood floors all throughout the cabin...*just stirring up the dust*, Bart thought. The twins especially enjoyed attacking dirt, stones, or bird droppings on the porch or sidewalk while the guys were outside working. Then they leaned their brooms upside-down against a railing and cried together, "Heads over Heels!" They left the brooms in the full sun for the day to disinfect the broom heads.

After Bart's morning school, he changed his hat from student to teacher. "Scoooo dime," Brinn shouted when she saw Bart's descent from the office upstairs.

"That's it, Brinn, school t-t-t-time," Bart enunciated specifically, repeating the "t" for emphasis. Steph had left lesson plans for Bart to help the twins learn number and letter recognition. Most of this work was actually games centered around Transformer Toys' names, colors, and Transformer activities in the Universe. Since the girls loved the T-toys so much, they were eager for these lessons, and Bart found he enjoyed their giddy recall of the education he was bringing them. *It's really cool to be a teacher,* Bart mused. He kept Cyber Stompin' Bumblebee on his desk and often pushed the fist to activate the flashing blue eyes and chest lights. Rather than creepy, there was something soothing about those blue eyes flashing at him. They reminded him of his Dad's azure blue eyes.

For lunch, the twins stirred up lemonade. They enjoyed trying out a sprig of different mint from the garden on each glass. They had enough choices for almost a week without a repeat: peppermint, pineapple mint, spearmint, lemon mint, apple mint, chocolate mint. "The wandering, insistent mint family has entertained homesteaders for eons," Steph had once said, although Bart remembered she hadn't seemed exactly happy with the tangled vines in the gardens.

The twins had learned good manners at home and routinely washed hands before, after, and during the lunch detail. They slapped together cold meat and cheese on sliced homemade bread (Steph had made several loaves and frozen them before she left for grad school. Then, Bart thawed and sliced what they needed day-by-day). The messiest sandwiches, but the most welcome when Uh-Oh was home, was peanut butter and jelly. The goo was slathered generously to the very edges of fat slices of bread by four little uncoordinated hands. "Heaven! Right here at my table," said Uh-Oh. Everyone smiled and sank into the deep sandwiches.

Afternoons on the homestead were usually outdoor work, play, or napping. Whenever someone was headed out after lunch, he or she yelled, "Roll out!" as a Transformer-style invitation, rallying the troops of sorts to the outdoors. Bart went to work at the various chores and upkeep required to maintain a homestead along with Uh-Oh or in his absence. The twins followed along and happily provided "gofer" work. Or they played at various safe sites, the porch, the flower garden, the gravel pile, or the hammock in the oak.

                         ঙঙঙ

Phone calls to Dad were more frequent. "Mom, when can I talk to Dad?"

"Bart, he's been asking the same for you, but he still can't talk for more than a couple minutes. Every time he wakes up, the first thing I see are his sparkling blue eyes…just like yours, honey. I miss you, too."

"Uh-uhm," Bart cleared his throat to keep from choking on a tear. "I thought he was getting better," he tried to not sound as exasperated as he was. He missed his dad and there was no denying it anymore. He wasn't too big to cry in bed at night for his dad or to cry after the nightmares. However, no one knew about this except Bart and his shelf full of Transformer Toys.

"Bart, tell me how you are doing and then let me talk to my baby girls."

"Well, the girls just lay down for a nap, but I can wake them."

"Oh no, I'll talk to them later…or maybe we can Skype. So tell me what's the latest on Uncle Owen's homestead."

"Oh, just stuff, Mom." Bart's voice was obviously dejected. Mom worried so she pushed.

"Like what stuff, honey?" Bart's sadness and weariness, fears, and missing home all jumbled together in his mind and so he spouted out a bit too loudly.

"I fix stuff, study stuff, mow stuff, hammer stuff, cook stuff, move stuff, build stuff…" Bart sucked in a guilty breath.

"Oh." Mom replied curtly, taken aback. "Bart, I'm sorry…"

"Mom, can I tell you more when I talk to Dad tonight? I'm…uh…I'm busy."

"OK, Bart." And they both hung up. Bart went to the barn and hammered nails into a cast-off 2x4 board. He hammered and hammered and hammered until his tears were all dried up and his prayers were all used up.

ソソソ

"Transformers, roll in!" Bart had made up the rallying cry to call the girls to bath time each evening. They always came giggling from whatever part of the yard or cabin they were playing. Now that they were "big girls," so they said, they didn't want Bart around during their bath/play time. Bart ran their tub water and filled it with bath toys. Then, he had at least 40 minutes of personal time while the girls bathed and played. They even took care of combing out each other's freshly shampooed hair. Bart heard a few "Owies!" but they tolerated each other and the necessary chore.

The twins came out of the bathroom with stringy, wet hair and scrubbed faces; both were wearing Bart's outgrown Transformer tee shirts. He loved snuggling them into their double bed and reading to them. Thanks to Steph, Bart had a list of suggested preschool stories to read at bedtime to the girls. The red-cheeked, plump little girls usually fell asleep before any story was finished. Tonight, Bart thought he heard a phone ring, but couldn't move to find the phone. He had fallen asleep at the foot of the girls' bed, the soft reading lamp blessing them all with a pink glow.

⌣⌣⌣

Bart and his sisters finally moved home the middle of November. The little girls were understandably clingy to Mom. And all Bart wanted to do was sit by Dad. Bart chose to continue with his online school, at least until the new year. And the twins were enrolled in a neighborhood preschool three half days each week. Mom worked fulltime those three days each week, Monday, Wednesday, and Friday. Bart shared the "man of the house" role with Dad.

One Wednesday morning Dad sat up in bed and said, "She's a beaut, this Ochre!" Bart was finishing a science assignment in the room next door.

"What did you say, Dad? Need something?" Bart walked into Dad's room and saw him fingering the tiny bell on the model pirate ship Bart had made for Dad's birthday.

"I said, 'She's a beaut, this Ochre!' Aye, Matey?"

"Aye, aye, sir." Bart saluted and smiled broadly. The pair fell to discussing the details of the ship, especially the handsome ochre paint. After just 20 minutes, Dad's voice faltered and he whispered.

"Sorry, Son. Pretty tired." He leaned back on his pillow and fell into a restless sleep. Bart set the ship on the bedside table and pulled the quilt to Dad's chin. Dad's face was pale yellowish. Bart prayed everyday for Dad's healing. *Recovery seems so slow*, he thought.

The twins came home from school and helped Bart start supper. "Ham, BoBo—I git it," said Betts.

"I git cheese," offered Brinn.

"How about if I spread mayo on the bread, Girls?"

"What else?"

"Let's get out chips and fruit, Twinsies." The girls brought out their little bench that Bart had made on the homestead. They pulled chips from the pantry shelf.

"Ooooooo! Stale berries!" squealed Brinn.

"Brinn, say straw – au-au – straw berries," corrected Bart, as he pulled them from the fridge. "What did you girls learn at school today?"

"Transformer Day!" the girls shouted in unison.

"Transformer Toys in preschool?" Bart asked.

"Yeth! Bumblebee!"

"Nooooo, Silwwy Sissy," one twin corrected the other. "We learned about bees, like beeee kind, beeee hopeful, beeee ratty…"

"Be ratty?" Bart had a hard time following their conversation.

"Yeth. Ratty to help, ratty to change, ratty to serve, ratty to go…"

"OK, you mean 'ready…' "

"Yeth. Ratty." The girls continued to chatter while they set the table with bowls and saucers. But Bart grabbed one preschool idea like a lifeline—"be hopeful, be ready to hope." Bart let hope stick in his brain and massage away every frightening thought about Dad. Bart let hope move to his heart and change his prayers from *Please, God, where are You?* to *I know You hear us and see us and care for us. Thank you.*

Just before Christmas Dad went to the hospital for an intestinal infection. Mom said it was "major." Uncle Owen came to stay with Bart's family, "for as long as you need me." Bart wanted to spend Christmas Eve Day with Dad. Mom and the girls went to the airport to get Steph and begin a day of cooking and baking. Uncle Owen dropped Bart off at the hospital, then went shopping. The whole family would all gather with a Christmas dinner in Dad's room the next day.

Bart opened the heavy drapes in Dad's room and winter sunlight flooded the corners of the dim, sterile place. The dull yellow, heavily starched blanket covering Dad turned golden. The glass vase of flowers on the counter sparkled, and the grey hair at Dad's temples twinkled as if the Twinsies had sprinkled glitter there. Dad put up his hand to shield his eyes and said, "Oh, it's Bart! I thought you were an angel in all that light!"

"Ha! I'm your Christmas angel, Dad!"

"Someone sure is! I've had a great night of sleep and good news from the docs this morning!" *Thanks, God,* Bart whispered. Dad tried to sit up but groaned. He pointed to the remote that operated the hospital bed.

Bart found the button to raise the top of the bed and fluffed Dad's sunken pillow.

"Thanks, Son. That feels better. Now, open the closet." Bart frowned but he opened the door where stood a box 20" x 20" x 10". Bart chuckled aloud. The picture on the big box displayed the newest giant transformer toy called Omega Supreme (O.S.).

"Merry Christmas, Son," Dad said.

"Dad, I... this transformer is so expensive...I mean, Dad..." Bart stuttered.

"Bart, your Uncle Owen and I have talked about your Universe of Transformers. This O.S. is a monster in size, yes, but he is powerful and most coveted of all the toys by the collectors. He stands for good and great power and always changes things for the better. He is a winner among Transformers!" Bart's face almost drained white, but his eyes were blue pools.

"Dad, I...I..."

"Bart, your mom and I...we love you so much...we can never thank you... we want you to know that you are our O.S."

Bart buried his face in Dad's neck and whispered, "Thanks, Dad." Dad hugged Bart weakly and said, "...good and great things, Son!" Bart chuckled and lifted his face to see Dad slowly close his tired, azure blue eyes.

"Take a nap, Dad. Love you!" Bart grabbed the box holding the giant Transformer and giddily tore into it.

Glossary and Story Questions

Open Season is originally a hunting term, meaning that any usual restrictions against hunting certain animals or with certain weapons or in certain areas are lifted. Likewise, Bart had offered his twin sisters to come to his room to play with the Transformer toys with the restriction of asking permission. But the little ones found it hard to be restricted in their supposed freedom to enter his room at will. Bart felt that the girls (hunters) could come and go and take what they wished whenever they wished, thus, "open season" on his room.

Transformer Toys were released in North America in 1984 with fifteen separate toy lines, various figures within each line and power status (technical specifications) or storylines to accompany each. Basically, the toy is molded for various parts that can shift about from a vehicle, a device, or an animal to a robot action figure and back again. All the toys are roughly divided into two main classifications: the Autobots who are the heroes who try to save the world from evil Decepticons. The Autobots may create alliances with humans for more intriguing play. All the action may take place with so many toys to create an entire "universe." The toylines progressed from 1984-2009, and there were a few movies, video games, cereals, events, and other items that were associated with Transformer Toys. A number of the individual toys or lines are named in this story.

Ships o' yore mean ships of yesteryears or ships from years gone by or long ago.

Belfry Ring A belfry is some structure that houses the bell, like the steeple in a church. On a ship, perhaps the belfry is a tower of sorts to allow the bell to be hung high off the deck and hang free to ring loudly. The belfry ring is the large heavy ring upon which a bell is hung, or, in this case of a model ship, it would be a small brass ring.

Ochre is pronounced "OH-ker" may be used as a noun, an adjective, or a verb. Generally, it has to do with colors ranging from yellow to deep orange or brown. It is (noun) a natural earth pigment containing hydrated iron oxide in the natural earth colors noted above and, as a noun, names the colors. As an adjective, ochre may describe the noun, "The oil spill created an ochre river." As a verb, ochre shows the action of something being colored with orange-browns. This word joins a number of other original French "loan words" that are accepted in the English language to be spelled with an "er" or "re" as in "theater/theatre." But such words are nonetheless pronounced as "er." It is interesting to search this topic and find the many examples of world languages borrowing from one another.

Barrels and Binnacle Barrels on ships of yore were generally yellow or brown wooden pieces: small barrels were called firkins and were used to store butter, while larger barrels called casks were used to store water or salt beef. Even larger barrels called tuns were used to store wine. The binnacle is about waist-high and is a housing for the ship's compass and perhaps other instruments for direction, speed, etc. The instruments are mounted on gimbals to keep the instruments true during the pitch and roll of the ship at sea.

∽∽∽

The following three "T" words are from Bart's middle school vocabulary test:

Thread a long, thin strand of fiber used in sewing or weaving; a thing that resembles a thread, especially due to its thinness; an ongoing conversation about one topic posted on the internet.

Texture the feel (rough or raised or frizzy or smooth), or appearance (bumpy, wavy, flat, etc.) of a surface or a substance.

Transform to make a thorough or dramatic change in the form, appearance, or character of. Synonyms for transform: change, alter, convert, metamorphose, transfigure, transmute, mutate.

Incredulous unwilling or unable to believe something. These sixth grade buddies may think they are a bit too cool to play with Transformer Toys, so, of course, they had to try to question and tease Bart about it. Here are a few interesting synonyms for "incredulous" that may give you a fuller idea of how these boys responded to Bart's mention of Transformer Toys: cynical, scorning, suspicious, goading.

Enunciated means that Bart spoke each letter and syllable correctly and clearly.

Canopy is usually a cloth covering, sometimes suspended

by poles, to protect or simply cover someone or something under it. In this case and often in poetic literature, a canopy may be the covering provided by foliage in the treetops.

Shooter Marbles Also called the "Boss" or "Taw", the shooter marble is used to play Ringer and other marble games. In official tournaments in the U.S., your shooter must be between 3/4" and 1/2" (quoted from the Moon Marble Company in Bonner Springs, Kansas).

Snood and Wattle are recognizable parts of a male turkey's head and chest. The long, red, fleshy area that grows from the forehead over the bill is a "snood," while the fleshy growth under the turkey's throat is called a "wattle." These pieces fill up with blood and turn bright red when a tom wants to attract a hen. However, they can also turn blue if the turkey is scared. If a turkey isn't feeling well, the snood and wattle become very pale.

At the Ready means to be prepared and available for immediate use.

Emblazoned means noticeably and conspicuously inscribed or displayed, perhaps as a design on something.

Flatware is also called "cutlery" or "table service," i.e., forks, spoons, knives, and other eating/serving utensils. Many years ago these pieces were made of silver, thus our word, "silverware." Now, most flatware is made of stainless steel.

Landline Does your family have a "landline?" It is

a phone in the home or business served by metal wire or fiber optic telephone lines. You may see some telephone lines as you drive down the road. Many people have left the telephone use of landlines and have only cell phones or phone capabilities on computers.

Livid has two meanings that could cooperate to offer a fuller description of the condition: (1) furiously angry and (2) a color of dark bluish gray. When your skin turns this color, it may be a bruise. Or the emotion of fury may be draining the blood from the face (usual pinkish or pale brown skin color).

Incoherent Synonyms are unclear, confused, unintelligible, not comprehending, hard to follow, disjointed, disconnected, mixed up, scrambled, and muddled.

Waxing Philosophical means wandering from a conversation of facts and figures to analyze meanings and larger purposes of life which may be suggested by the topic at hand.

Pig on the Spit Bart's uncle was roasting a pig during an all-day affair for a pork supper. The pig, or whatever part of the pig desired to be roasted, is hung from or by a spit which is a long metal rod(s) suspended over a low burning fire. The meat must be turned often/continuously either by hand-crank or by electronic rotisserie. YUM!

Fatback is fat from the upper part of a side of pork, often made into bacon and especially, the fat may be dried and salted in strips.

Homesteading A little history: In the 1860s a law was passed to encourage Americans to help settle the Western United States, truly, the wild West. Anyone 21 years old or older, including freed slaves, were offered a free title for 160 acres of land if they would improve it and live on it for at least five years. You can imagine all the hard work:

- Haul family and household goods and food (not in cars but in covered wagons and not on paved roads but across rugged terrain, streams, mountains)
- Drive animals the days or months or years required to leave the East to the offered region
- Scout for acreage close to a water source (stream, river, pond)
- Clear the land of rocks, unwanted trees, forests, underbrush
- Build a home and outbuildings (no construction crew)
- Heat the home (no furnaces)
- Haul water daily
- Break (literally) ground for building and crops
- Plant gardens (no grocery stores!!)
- Care of animals
- Protection of property
- Home crafts, foods, services for trading
- Socialization (protective cooperation) with Indians or other settlers

Modern homesteading is more like a lifestyle of self-sufficiency. It requires a belief that you and your family have the ability to mostly provide for yourselves and not to have to depend on others. Homesteading requires that you live closely from the land and create a healthy land, community, and personal lives that will sustain you and your dependents. Key practices of homesteaders:

- Personal (or family) freedom
- Subsistence, organic agriculture, cooperate with the "original" design of nature
- Heirloom vegetables and heritage livestock, hearty and hardy beginnings and propagating of plants
- Home preservation of foodstuffs, home remedies and health enhancements
- Small-scale textiles, craftwork, or other businesses that support the homestead
- Renewable energy such as solar electricity and wind power
- Minimal connection with mass integration

Board Ripping means to split or saw timber in the direction of the grain, keeping the resulting board rather free from splintery fibers and producing a flat board. Knots may be managed also by ripping the board rather than splitting along the grain (riven).

Challenge (see "Ochre"): Can you think of any word you often use that is **borrowed from another language**? Ask a teacher or parent to name one!!

Why do you think **Bart refers to his dad as "the ship's bell"** in the first chapter, in paragraph #6?

Can you do a ten-minute search on the internet about your **favorite toy(s)** and write a paragraph like the one above about Transformers?

See the definition of **"incredulous." Tell about a time** you may have felt teased, scorned, or goaded among friends?

List three interesting **experiences Bart had during the car trip** to the homestead, "from the east side of Indiana to the west side of Illinois."

Ready, Set, Stretch!! Bart went through a **series of stretches** to help his achy muscles when he first started working at the homestead. Follow Uncle Owen's instructions and try to do two of each exercise. Now, how does that feel?

What are a few things that Bart learned to do on the **homestead that are not usually taught in public school**?

What thing did **Bart have to keep reminding people**, which seemed to irritate him?

Class project: Divide class into seven research groups; each group studies, then creates a poster or other media presentation per each of the **seven key practices** of homesteaders. Homeschoolers may be interested in applying such a project to key practices or values among local homeschooling advocates.

Slippery Rock

for Izzy

Anders[†] bit her hanging fingernail and spit it in the brass pot where the giant silk palm tree stood. The elevator door opened. Smooth jazz music swelled out and the girl rushed in. She couldn't be late again for the trolley to school.

But she was. So she walked down Seventh Avenue toward Advante Middle School, uncaring really that she'd have to explain to the principal…again. *Mom's ill, the cat got out of the condo, the trolley forgot to stop…I'll think of something,* she mused. She felt that ragged fingernail snag at her sheer shirt and so chewed at the nail again, spitting this time onto the boardwalk bench.

Anders noticed a brilliant gleam flashing two blocks ahead and hurried toward it. The sun was shining on a bright brass nameplate of an art sculpture. She stopped and tried to glare back up at the sun, but it hurt her eyes. She squeezed them shut, and a fragrance fell over her like a party dress. A profusion of gardenias hung over the fence just behind her. She pulled out her nail clippers and snipped off a showy spray. Now, she'd be late to fifth grade for sure.

"He loves me, he loves me not; he loves me, he loves me not, he loves me…" she stopped pulling and dropping the gardenia petals as she walked and said rather loudly, "Well, of course he does!" But, of course, she didn't really know if her daddy loved her. She didn't know him at all. He was only one big fat wish in her heart.

Anders saw a single stone on the well-swept sidewalk and kicked it a bit harder than necessary. She ran to it and kicked again. She kicked and kicked all four blocks to Advante, no matter if several times the stone scuffed parked car doors and sidewalk planters. She picked up the little stone and dropped it into her backpack. A lone slightly wilty gardenia stem would have to be her transgression[†] present to Ms. Alos.

"But this progress report is not showing much progress, Andi," Mom complained, as if the school tardiness really DID bother her. "And, your principal just called to be sure I got the report. Why would the school think you wouldn't bring me the report? Anders?"

"Ms. Alos called you? Oh, boy. OK, sorry, Mom, I'll do better."

"You'll have to because I cannot take off work to make sure you are at school on time. I always wake you in time for school, and the trolley is dependable..." And this is where Anders checked out. She stared at Mom solemnly as Mom's black eyes flashed and her face pinched. But Anders was really sizing up Mom's good looks rather than listening. Alternately, Anders gazed into the mirror in her head to study her own looks, then back to her mom: She imagined her own glistening green eyes and reddish freckles, her mom's dark golden skin and wide nose, her own straight blonde bob, her mom's cocoa brown tightly curled hair. Surely, she thought, her dad would be a composite† of the two gals. Anders drifted off to her room.

Anders had more clothes on the bedroom floor than those in her still-stuffed-full closets. She kicked the outfits around wondering why her mom didn't clean up once in a while. Her toe bumped the little prism hiding beside the foot of her bed. She set it on the slate-gray painted windowsill, remembering her favorite lesson in science class last year. The only reason Anders knew the name of the paint on the windowsill was because painting her windowsill was her biggest punishment ever! Just because she had marked on the window casing with pencil and engraved a couple doodles on the sill...well, she just couldn't get her mom to understand that she had not really hurt anything, "It IS my own windowsill, isn't it?!" she had argued with Mom. But then...Anders got to pick out whatever color she wanted for the job. No matter the whole room was a soft robin egg blue, now, her own window casing was a smoky dark gray-blue. She liked it and that's all that matters, *right? Right?* she challenged her conscience.[†]

The prism looked like a crystal pyramid sitting there. The sun sank slowly down and shot through the neighboring high-rise buildings. She kneeled, staring at the prism, and nibbled at the crooked thumbnail until it happened: "Magic!" she whispered. The seven-pronged rainbow slowly spread across one wall. Anders grabbed the little kicking stone from her backpack and set it on the windowsill beside the prism. She sat very still. She glared at the beauty. She nibbled her thumb again. As the sun finally dropped and the rainbow disappeared, she spit a piece of thumbnail toward the window, but the screen caught it and bounced back into the window track.

Her phone sang "...*calling, calling, calling me home*..." from the *Lights* cut by Great Britain's pop singer Ellie Goulding. Anders didn't understand the song lyrics at all, but since her BFF's name was also Ellie...*well, why not*, she thought when she linked the song tone to Ellie's name in her phone. Anders let Ellie go to voice mail. *She doesn't really, really get me, anyway. Probably just bragging about that Vermont trip with her dad,* Anders thought. In spite of herself, Anders listened to Ellie's message,

"So...don't forget we are bus buddies tomorrow on our Nature Field Trip," Ellie was blabbering. "I'm wearing my new One-Stars and my pink bomber jacket. You? Oh, and....wait 'til you see what Dad got me in Vermo..." Anders snapped off her phone. *Ellie's bragging, I can do without, but the nature walk? I'm all in!!* Anders mused.

Anders pulled the quilt to her chin, but suddenly remembered the mail Mom had slipped under her door.

Three pieces: the first mailer was a flier for Tweens Cupcake Night at the teahouse at Kyoto Lawns. And another was yet another invitation to join AARP. *When will they ever realize that I am an 11-year-old-girl, not an old man?!* Anders rolled her eyes and ripped the envelope in half; she bent her wrist and spun the two pieces of the envelope toward her trash can like a Frisbee gone awry. She glanced down at her final piece of mail. "Mama Metta!" Anders squealed aloud. She restrained herself from tearing into the manila envelope from her dear grandmother. Mama Metta lived in Visby, Sweden, the only town on an island province. As a very young child, Anders stayed on the island with Metta for an entire summer. She learned to love Metta deeply and now Anders missed her constantly. Anders smoothed her hand over the handwritten face like petting a "kattunge," Swedish for a very tiny kitten. She smelled the back of the envelope where her grandmother would have pressed and then kissed the closure. Anders would savor every moment with Mama Metta.

Metta had promised to write to Anders about her "papa…someday, when right time," her grandmother had often said. Every week, Anders hoped that Metta would finally realize this is the right time. Instead, again this week Mama Metta sent more charcoal sketches of her beloved homeland: the dashing hills and windy trees, the foamy seas. Metta printed a simple message, usually some little life lesson to her granddaughter, "Kind and pure you must be, Andres. To nature, be good." Metta always called Anders "Andres."

"Andres, you lovely bloom. You not manly," Metta had said. "Anders means manly. A son, your papa wanted a son. He was wrong, my son wrong to give you manly name. A lovely girl, my girl you are, Andres.[†]"

Anders squeezed away hot tears. She scraped the flaking indigo polish off her pinky. She flipped the chips onto the floor mixed with Forever21, Lululemon, and PacSun.[†] She carefully refolded the letter, stuffed it into the envelope, and slipped it under her pajama shirt. She slept fitfully but with Mama Metta's letter next to her heart.

∽∽∽

Waiting for the trolley to school this morning wasn't nearly as thrilling as waiting in line after first period for the bus to Clark's Nature Center. Ellie was fourth in line and called out to Anders to cut in with her. Several other fifth graders frowned; some attempted, "Hey, you…" but Anders stuck out her tongue at them, showing off her wad of pink bubble gum.

"Where's your One-Stars, Anders?" asked Ellie showing off her new teal ones.

"I thought hiking through woods full of damp moss and dirt called for practical brown hiking boots," Anders chewed the big wad of gum harder. She looked all around the playground to avoid eye contact with Ellie, showing irritability toward her friend.

"Oh." Ellie looked crestfallen[†] and turned slowly around to face the bus door which began to open.

Ms. Johns, the science teacher, leaned against the dashboard talking to the bus driver. Anders spit her gum onto the pavement at the bottom step before she boarded the bus. "Hey, stop!" The bus driver held out her meaty arm at Anders and grabbed a tissue with her other hand, "Clean it up," she told Anders, while the science teacher just stared wide-eyed at her student. The line of fifth graders pressed forward.

"What? What are you talking about?" Anders looked and sounded so innocent and she may have been deemed so had not the science teacher taken the bus driver's side.

"Anders!" said the surprised teacher and then to the queue, "Back up, Everybody, back up a step or two. There's a clean up here!" She shooed the kids back like a flock of chickens.

Kids stepped backwards with the occasional, "OW! Off my feet…" Anders grabbed the tissue and jumped from the top bus step onto the pavement with one leap and a livid face. She scooped up the offensive pink blob, squeezed the tissue around it, enjoying the squishy give-and-take of the mass inside her hand. Anders stomped back up the steps and to the seat Number 22 beside Ellie. Seat 22: the dark green vinyl seat covering was inked with decades of graffiti. There was a split in the middle of the seat revealing a puke-yellow colored foam cushion underneath. Anders, teeth gritted, peeled off a strip of vinyl widening the crack by two inches. She then tore the strip into tiny deep green pieces and threw them in the air like confetti. Ellie knew better than to speak at that moment.

At the second intersection, Ms. Johns stood at the front of the bus and shushed the students. She had regained her cheery disposition, "Well, Class, we're off to see the _____."
Here, Ms. Johns purposely paused awaiting someone to fill in the blank.

"…wizard! The wonderful wizard of Oz!" yelled one particularly nerdy boy.

"OOOO, love that movie!" Ellie giggled.

"Welllllll, OK," said Ms. Johns never losing opportunity to encourage any student. "Yes, let's say we are off to see the wizard of Clark's Nature Center!!! And he is sitting right here!!" Ms. Johns' enthusiasm was wasted on Anders. "Stand up, Noel, and tell us the rules about our hike today."

"Rules? Did she say rules?" whispered Anders to anyone around her. "Really? There are rules for walking through the woods? The outdoors is there for everybody, right?" Kids around her humphed and ha-ha-ed, influenced by her disrespectful scorn.

"Hi, Guys. I'm Noel Clark, third-generation keeper of the nature center. You'll be doing more than just walking through woods today. I hope that's OK. We'll be checking badger tunnels, counting cubs in their setts,[†] and identifying various bugs. We'll also scoop some tadpoles from the pond. I'll pass out a paper here about the rules or reminders of etiquette[†] in the wild. Hey, Young Man…" Noel handed a stack to the teacher's pet who always managed to sit right next to Ms. Johns. "Pass these back and each one take one, please."

"Etiquette? What is this? Be nice to the animals and trees, huh, Anders?" Ellie scoffed. But Anders was already studying the paper.

Welcome to Clark's Nature Center
Friendly Reminders

Safety First!
Remember your surroundings. This is the home of birds, animals, water creatures, and even insects. Stay on the paths – you may get lost or injured among the underbrush. Watch your step – there are uneven

walking trails. Respect other people who want to enjoy the green space and the relative stillness here.

Hike on the Right, Pass on the Left

Hiking a trail may be like driving a car on the road. Please keep to the right when you are being passed. When you want to pass someone from behind, you might shout out, "On your left."

Tech on the Trail

School classes are asked to refrain from taking any digital devices on their educational visits to the hiking trail or the nature center. For all other visitors, please be courteous regarding the space or noise that may accompany taking pictures and posting them, listening to music or answering phone calls, etc.

Leave No Trace

This is an important rule of visiting natural and preserved green spaces. The most important way to "leave no trace" is to clean up after yourself. Please pack out anything and everything that you brought in. The only animals the public may bring onto our grounds are service animals.[†] If you visit with one, you must clean up after your animal. Another way to "leave no trace" is to stay on the trail. Not only might you get lost if you leave the trail, but also you will damage fragile plants, erode trails, and loosen rocks and boulders that may injure you or people on trails below you. Finally, you are prohibited from taking any part of our property: a leaf, a bug, a rock, a flower, a stick. Every tiny single item in the green space is part of the whole ecosystem. Please do not upset it. The only exception, of course, is when students are instructed to participate in the landscape by tour guides.

Gift Shop

A variety of symbolic and crafted items representing many lovely pieces and places of the grounds are available in the gift shop. The minimal prices allow provision for continuous improvement and maintenance of the nature center.

Ms. Johns was standing and thanking Mr. Clark when the bus jerked forward. She fell against him and he caught her in an embrace. The students as a whole grinned and hissed out, "wooooo-hooooo" or with their hands over their mouths, "ohmmmmmmm!" Anders rolled her eyes and bit the last of her index cuticle, spitting it into the hair of the girl in front of her.

∽∽∽

Anders had never heard of trail etiquette. Actually, she had few manners at all, in particular for outdoor or public places. Anders imagined most of the world was her own. Certainly, her own home and apartment building were her own, she thought. But the Etiquette Paper that Noel Clark handed out was sticking with Anders...actually, it was sticking its nose[†] right into her entire understanding of the world.

After hiking quietly in a line with the students for only ten minutes, Anders felt her eyes water and her nose fill up. *Pollen, I guess*, she thought. She blew her nose on a tissue and absently dropped it on the trail. She was captivated by her first sight of a waterfall far ahead. A kid behind her let out a self-righteous shout, "EWWWEEWWW!" Anders turned to see the kid pointing to the tissue. She grabbed it up and stared nose-to-nose with the whiny little kid, and stuffed it into her pocket with venom.

Anders followed the crowd, staying to the right and passing on the left...she passed a bit too often and with a gruff, "move over!" Anders had managed to ditch Ellie. She only wanted to concentrate on the natural beauty around her, not understanding but liking the feeling of wonder that often overtook her while in nature. At one point, she felt that her Mama Metta would nearly be in tears at the beautiful woodsy sights. Anders felt a lump rise up so quickly into her throat that she gagged and spit into the side of the trail. Another wail, "Ewwweewww" arose behind her and she sprinted off to close in on the waterfall.

A knot[†] of fifth-graders hung to the railing around the 40-foot waterfall, occasional splashes spraying their faces and shoes. Anders heard giggling and what she imagined was laughter, lyrical laughter. But the kids were passively enjoying the sights. *What is that sound? The crowd, the water?* Anders listened and looked, listened and looked, but she seriously could not decide. She saw a thin path leading further down to the pond at the bottom of the waterfall. She left the crowd and felt deliciously like she was sneaking away. Anders always liked to feel like she was getting away with something…even though she always began biting her nails upon such expeditions.

There were only three kids stooping at the edge of the pond. Noel Clark was showing them how to dip in a net and where to catch the tadpoles, "…they love to hide under the shale.[†] Notice the several layers of this jagged rock? It gives the baby frogs places to wiggle into. They swim to deep or shallow places, as they wish."

"It reminds me of the poolside at our apartment building," Teacher's Pet said.

Anders wasn't interested in the tadpoles, but certainly liked the stacked skinny rocks bordering the pond. They were blue-gray in color, exactly the color of her bedroom window casing. The stones were flat and layered with chipped off pieces here and there. *What did Mr. Clark call them? Shale? Yeah! Shale-gray! Makes sense!*

Most of the shale pieces were larger than the school

lunch tray but a few were just the size of Anders' hand, just the size to be slipped secretly into her backpack. *What a beautiful rock to sit on my windowsill – a rock colored exactly the same as my sill!! Coool!* Anders thought. She stooped and turned her back to Noel and the other kids. She slowly put her fingers into the pond and touched the edge of a small shale. Suddenly she lost sense of anyone around her as she felt the cool rush of the water against her skin. She wiggled her fingers and felt the moving currents massage and squeeze each fingertip. The feeling was tantalizing. Touching the ragged-edged stone with the water rushing through her fingers was irresistible. Suddenly, she was aware of vibrations or...was it humming? Was she feeling a melody or hearing one? Or perhaps someone's phone was ringing a tune. She wasn't sure. She looked around and no one was reaching for their device. And no one was watching her. Everyone else seemed as calm and fascinated looking at nature as Anders was touching it.

ɔɔɔ

Anders felt transported after two hours in the wild—the sparkly waterfall, the flipping tadpoles in the beaker of pond water, the three badger cubs pawing at the ground for bugs, the giant butterflies, the calling, swooping birds...and no Ellie. *I'm a new girl!* she imagined. And she was! That is...she thought she was until the class lined up for the bus to return to Advante...and when Ellie found her. Ellie began to berate all the dirty, silly activities of the day, "And, my One-Stars are ruined!" she lamented.

"They looked like moss when you came and they look

like moss going home—what's the big deal?" spouted Anders at her BFF. Oh, how quickly and how far Anders fell from delight to disgruntled![†]

It wasn't only hiking back toward the fifth grade group and Ellie that irritated Anders, but also she was feeling nervous. Her ragged index fingernail sent her on a chewing frenzy. Furthermore, Anders started thinking about her papa again. She wondered if he liked the outdoors. Maybe she even got her love for the wild from Papa. The more she walked the return hilly path, the more unsettled her heart felt. Anders' nose was still full, her eyes burning, *Why the snot? From the pollen? Or is it all my questions about Papa?* Her heart felt guilty, lonely, and heavy.

In addition, her backpack had gotten quite soaked and was dripping into her jeans. As Anders took her place miserably in line, she noisily wadded up the Etiquette Paper from Noel Clark and threw it toward the trash receptacle where the students deposited their lunch sacks. She missed and she didn't care. "He loves me not," she whispered hoarsely.

In Seat 22 Anders again picked at the vinyl seat crack absently. She found she had ripped off a hunk of vinyl the size of a Father's Day card. Ellie's eyes grew wide. Anders aimed and pitched the piece out of the window like a Frisbee.

At home, Anders dropped all her clothes and hiking gear into the kitchen corner near the laundry chute. She took a hot shower and crawled into bed early. "Honey, are you OK?" Mom asked when she got home at 8.

"Big hiking day. Tired, Mom."

"Well, OK, but did you spill something in the kitchen? Everything is wet around your clothes."

"My backpack got pretty soaked. Sorry." Anders shouted. "I'll get it tomorrow."

"Any papers in your backpack I need to see, honey?"

Anders gave a shrill whine, "Geesh, Mom! I'm too tired right now. Let me sleep." The girl began to drift toward sleep but then, a sudden full-body jerk. Anders' brain kicked in with, *Ohhhhhhh nooooo! I should get up and grab that shale before Mom throws everything down the chute to the basement laundry room. I should get up, I should get up, I should get…*but Anders couldn't move one muscle and couldn't think one more thought.

When morning broke and Anders woke, she bolted up thinking only of her shale. She jumped from the bed to the bedroom door in one leap. Rounding the hall to the kitchen, she found all her clothes gone and her hiking boots sitting on newspapers. "Noooo, oh noooo…!! Where's my backpack?" she squealed toward the kitchen ceiling, but then Anders spied it hanging on the kitchen doorknob. There was a mixing bowl on the floor just below it, collecting a steady drip from the backpack. And there was a note clipped to the zipper pull,

I am not looking in here - it stinks.
Clean it out today B4 you go to school!!
Luv u

Although Anders made fun of her mom's shorthand, "B4" for "before," at least Mom didn't find her secret! Anders plucked out her shale which was sitting in five inches of water. *Wow, didn't know my backpack held that much water!!* Anders wondered. She grabbed a paper towel and dabbed at the shale all the way to her bedroom windowsill. She gently set the shale on the sill. *There you go! Shale on shale!* Anders suddenly felt as happy as she did at the pond. She gently patted the shale like a puppy's head and saw a tiny splat when her fingers touched the cold rock. "Sun and today's breeze will dry you out. See ya later!" Anders said to her pet shale as she turned to jump into school clothes. She still had twenty-five minutes. Plenty of time!

Anders grabbed yoghurt and a granola bar while she fluffed her hair and tied her One-Stars, *Today's a smarter day to wear my Chucks*, she thought, disparaging Ellie's choice from yesterday. Thinking of Ellie, she wondered if she was hearing her "*...calling, calling, calling me home...*" ringtone in the bedroom. Her phone was on the bedside table, but there was no light flashing and no vibration and no music coming from it. *Maybe some app update tone*, Anders guessed. As she left her room, she noted a streak of dark blue running down the wall below the window. A second glance showed that there was a little puddle under the shale and was just beginning to overflow the sill onto the wall paint. *Wow, I didn't get that shale dry, did I!* and she wiped the wall with a smelly ankle sock she found under her dresser. The matching sock was on the arm of her comfy chair, so she grabbed that as a coaster for her shale pet to rest on all day. As Anders left the apartment, she thought she heard her phone ring again, but an unfamiliar tone, an odd tone like an hour-chime clock with a wearing-out battery. *What could that be?* but she listened again in frozen silence at the open apartment door. The slight screeching tone began again, nearly incomprehensible; she strained to listen to the screech she thought may be coming from her room. But suddenly the elevator door opened in the hallway and Anders had to run out to the trolley.

಩಩಩

Fifth grade demanded everything Anders could give today. She didn't think about her pet shale all day long. She didn't even think about it all evening since she had attended the Cupcake Night at Kyoto's. When she got home Anders was so tired she just wanted to fall into bed. She hurried through the dark apartment and stepped over to her bedroom window to pat her pet shale goodnight. One foot slipped on wet carpet and the other landed in a virtual pool under the sill. Cool water squeezed through Anders' toes. She yelped and jumped backwards instinctively. Disoriented, she tripped over scattered clothes and shoes as she scrambled toward the light switch.

The shale was producing its own tiny fountain! Sparkling water drops pushed out of several layers of the chipped rock. *Looks like it's sweating*, Anders wondered. She stared in amazement. Then she heard an undeniable sound that she felt certain was coming from the shale. The sound was faint but reminded her of pulling a drinking straw up and down, up and down through the tight lid hole in a soft drink cup. It was a squealing sound, a teeny, tiny screaming sound, a pitiful sound.

Hmmmm, I didn't think rocks stay wet all the time...nor did I know they can cry!? Ha! Anders chuckled at her own ridiculous thoughts. Yet, this was all so confusing and unsettling. She decided the shale wasn't such a great souvenir, after all. So she threw it into the metal bathroom trash can. All night long Anders heard a faint *BUBBLE-PING, BUBBLE-PING, BUBBLE-PING*, a sort of tinny sound. She dreamed about swimming in the shale pool at Clark's Nature Center. She was tiny as the tadpoles. The shale rocks seemed to be singing to each other. Fountains of water sprayed all around her. It was happy water. She felt happy.

Anders awoke the next morning hearing Mom grumble under her breath, "Whaa...whaaat is this? Who spilled something in the bathroom can?" There was water seeping out the bottom seams of the metal can. "Anders! Anders, honey, wake up! Time to get up. Please empty the bathroom trash; I gotta get to work!" And she left the apartment.

Anders jumped out of bed and ran to the bathroom. There was water pooling around the trash can. She didn't want to believe it could be her discarded rock, but when she opened the lid, there floated the shale on top! She jumped back, now afraid. *I better call Mom about this weird rock.* But then decided, *No, then I'd have to explain the water stain on my bedroom carpet and on my windowsill. I'll just get rid of this thing for good!* So Anders jerked the trash bag liner out of the metal can and began to run to the back patio. The bag dripped all the way. She noticed a sharp point of the shale had ripped a little hole in the bag. Anders threw the bag into the patio corner and water gushed out of the mouth and over the side of the porch. She returned to MOP-MOP-MOP the bathroom with dry bath towels. She pitched the wet ones down the laundry chute and reinserted a clean trash liner into the can. *Finally! OK! Done! That is that!* she thought.

But getting ready for school, Anders heard that odd, tinny noise again that she recalled from last night. She checked her still-damp windowsill, the metal trash can in the bathroom, and then opened the mouth of the liner bag on the patio. The tiny, tinny, squeaky, squealing, piercing sound came from the bag; specifically, it seemed to arise from the edge of the shale. *CREEEEEPY!* The word slithered out on the girl's hot breath. The hairs on Anders' arms lifted. Her neck prickled, and her armpits itched. She backed into the house, locked the patio door, and turned on her loudest music.

∽∽∽

Anders wondered if her head had filled with bumblebees with all the thoughts buzzing and bumping into each other. She covered her ears and refused to think one more shale thought as she got ready for school. But at her desk during first period, Anders could think of nothing else except the shale. Through all seven periods, Anders' mind raced back and forth like a ping-pong game. She wished the garbage truck to appear today and take away this problem, but she knew the truck wasn't due until Saturday. She imagined an extra large city pigeon might zoom onto the patio and scoop up the trash bag and fly it to Never-Never Land. But in her mind that became a ridiculous cartoon. Anders even strategized, *Perhaps if I think hard enough, if I wish long enough, a daylight robber might climb up the three stories of patios and steal that trash bag.* By the end of the day, Anders' head was pounding.

Back in the apartment building after school, Anders cautiously, quietly stuck only her head into the apartment. All appeared calm. She tiptoed toward the patio, slipping first behind the hutch, out of sight-line to the patio, and then ducked behind the sofa, listening hard, straining to hear anything out of the ordinary. She peeked around corners and over end tables, moving slowly toward the patio like a prowling animal. Anders could see no change in the position of the bag; she saw no movement within the bag and could hear no sounds coming from the patio. She began to relax. Approaching the patio door, she was relieved to see that there was no dripping or even wet stains around the bag. She had had enough of this adventure and laughed at herself for all her whirlwind fears. But still, she checked the lock on the patio door—twice—and then quickly closed the drapery. "Yep, that is that!" she said out loud and let herself giggle.

But, at suppertime, when Mom came home, she asked, "Hey, sweetie! Did it sprinkle here this afternoon? There is a little stream of water running past the parking garage." Anders bolted to the patio. She saw that the bottom of the bag was leaking through the space between the floorboards onto the patio below, and the patio below that, and even onto the first-floor patio below that. The leaking had created a very tiny stream that ran down the sidewalk and along the parking garage. A jagged corner of the shale stuck up through the mouth of the bag, and the tiniest bubbles Anders had ever seen popped on the edge, letting out a tiny lip-smacking sound. This time rather than fear, Anders felt pity for the lonely shale. *What else can it be?* Anders wondered in awe. *My pet rock is crying. And I must be crazy!*

Anders picked up the little rock and laid it gently into the flowerpot in the opposite corner of the patio. She walked back to her bedroom, dragging her feet, stunned really. She didn't even hear Mom ask her what she wanted for supper. Anders shut her bedroom door and immediately called Mama Metta, for Mama Metta knows all things.

"Oh, Sondotter...or, how you say? Ah, yah, my granddaughter. Ha! Big story you tell. Wise questions. Wise heart. Have no fear." Mama Metta talked a long while explaining her own beliefs about the natural world, "Truth in nature, Sondotter, spirit in nature." Metta told Anders the many ways that nature is honored and celebrated in her own homeland. She reminded Anders that animals and living things share our space in the world, our water, our air. She talked about respect for all things. Anders suddenly remembered her own spitting, littering, and stealing at the nature center. She felt her cheeks flame and the breath sucked out of her. She actually looked around to see if anyone caught her rehearsing her own disrespect for all things.

"Spirit, everywhere, Andres. Life, many forms, many places, in all things. Be Wise, my Andres! Honor all life."

"But Metta, rocks crying? Can rocks cry?"

"Oh, darling! The histories of the peoples of the world are captured in the hills and rocks of the Earth. Yes, rocks speak, they teach. Why not weep? They may laugh, too!" And here Mama Metta let out a hearty hoot. It sounded like a pure laugh full of joy.

"OK, Metta, I have to go tell Mom everything. But while I have you on the phone, I'm ready to talk about Papa…" but Metta had already hung up, laughing a real laugh.

It was sunset when Noel Clark opened the gate at Clark's Nature Center. He smiled at Anders and Mom. He handed Mom a large gas lantern and pointed out the path to the waterfalls. He gently patted the hand-sized grey shale Anders carried, then disappeared into his office.

Mother and daughter walked soberly hand-in-hand down the beautiful, fragrant, dusky pathways. A full moon

arose and was caught as if scribbled light in the wavy waterfall. There were laughing, singing waters; yes, Anders actually heard the joyful waters abandoning themselves over the cliff, sparkling their way down, down, down to the pool with splashes, little and large. She heard contagious laughter at each splash.

Mom followed Anders down a steep, rutted path to the pool. Neither could speak for the lump in her throat. The night was hushed, but nature was resounding. The rocks at the edge of the pool seemed to shift and clatter; the shale in Anders' hand grew warm and trembled. She laid it on the brim of the pool, against a shale shelf. Tadpoles popped in and out of the water. Little fish seemed to stop in place and shake only their shimmery tails causing tiny whirlpools to rush over the shale family. Iridescent bubbles arose and floated on the top of the pool, swirling in the moonlight. And Mom gasped.

"Did you hear that, Anders?" She whispered. "Did you hear the laugh? Nature laughs!"

Anders dropped her face into her hands and quietly wept. Or was she giggling? She couldn't tell. Mom draped an arm around Anders' shoulder and kissed the top of her head, "Kattunge," Mom whispered. "This is a special moment for us, isn't it? There are so many things in my heart." Anders looked up into her mom's pooling dark eyes. "I've been wanting to talk to you for a long time about something… about your papa…"

Glossary and Story Questions

Anders/Andres In Scandinavian languages Anders is usually a boy's name and means manly or brave. It is similar to Andreas in Greek and Andrew in English (British). Anders has been a popular name in Sweden for hundreds of years. In the Spanish language the equivalent name is Andres.

Transgression means going beyond a boundary, either a law or an expectation or a physical barrier. Examples: In a flood, a river transgresses its banks; a cheating student transgresses school rules; a sinner is one who breaks God's rules. A marriage partner who gives illicit affection to someone outside the marriage transgresses the marital vows.

Composite is a whole thing made up of (adj.) various parts. Anders was wondering what her dad may look like and figured her own looks and her mom's looks put together may give her a clue of her dad's looks.

Conscience is a human feeling, an inner understanding, suggestion, voice that may act as a guide as to the rightness or wrongness of one's own behavior.

Forever21, Lululemon, and PacSun are expensive and popular clothing brands especially targeting tween girls. Since Anders has many of these clothes strewn all about her bedroom and stuffed in her closets, what might you guess about her family economy and her own attitude toward the family economy?

Crestfallen means disappointed or dejected or embarrassed. See if you can find at least five other synonyms to get a good picture of Ellie's response to Anders' unkind words.

Setts This interesting word, usually in the plural as you see it here, is used to describe at least four very different things. Following you will read four meanings of the word. Please choose the one that seems to fit this story.

- a small, rectangular granite or quarried paving stone
- the pattern of stripes in a tartan
- the lair or burrow of a badger
- the number of warp threads per inch or centimeter on a loom

Etiquette means good manners, polite behavior, expected behavior or rules of conduct among certain clubs, groups, professionals, etc.

Service Animals usually refer to dogs that assist disabled persons for a number of reasons, sometimes for aiding sight, sometimes for recognizing the onset of a medical emergency, such as epilepsy, etc.

Stick Its Nose This idiom means to show too much interest in a business or situation that does not involve you. It is usually considered rude to ask too many questions about or try to involve yourself in someone else's personal life. Do you think that Anders understood the rules of etiquette from the nature center might suggest good manners she could apply to other areas in her life?

Knot in this story means a small group of people clustered together. Can you describe another kind of knot?

Shale soft, fine sedimentary rock. It is formed from compacted mud or clay. It can be split easily into breakable thin pieces.

Disgruntled means discontented, resentful, disappointed, angry, dissatisfied.

〰〰〰

Anders might be an unusual name to you. Discuss **your own given name** with your family to find out where it came from. If there was any other name you could choose for yourself, what would it be? And what does it mean?

Do you know anyone who has **a habit of chewing fingernails?** Perhaps this habit might indicate the person is _____. After reading the whole story, do you think the word you wrote might describe Anders? Why or why not?

Anders is curious about or yearns for **information about her "papa" or her dad**. Can you find all the places in this story that suggest Anders' quest? There are at least eight!

List some of Anders' behaviors that you consider **poor manners**. Name a few **good manners** you have. (Here's a good manner that is especially nice: When a young girl or boy says "Yes, ma'am" to adults.)

How did Anders' adventure with the shale lead her to consider her **grandmother's beliefs about the natural world.**

Investigate what **beliefs your own ancestors may have had about the natural world.** Do you agree or disagree with them?

Is there some **mysterious thing in nature** that interests you or one you have researched or discussed with others?

Find **references to "light"** whether a natural light, a reflective light, an indoor light, or the light in a character's mind that came with new understanding.

Underground

for Owen

A rley carried the last box from the moving van, toward his new house. He held an open cardboard box with a couple of Mom's heavy medical texts, mismatched shoes, tangled clothes hangers, and a couple packages of light bulbs. Arley noticed the bulbs were busted to pieces. He didn't mind that. He got a big shock once as a kid trying to replace a light bulb. He hasn't trusted them ever since.

It was 3 p.m., the hottest part of the summer day. His family had been working with the movers since 8 a.m. Sweat stung Arley's eyes and his shorts stuck to his rump. The moving van pulled away after a mover carelessly dropped a full-page bill-of-sale onto Arley's open box. August 26, it read. But Arley calculated in his head, *Wait! August 26? Today isn't the 26'th! Let's see…school starts Tuesday the 30th so today is…today is Thursday, August 25!* "Professional incompetence!†" Arley muttered, sounding very much like his dad.

A high-pitched scritch-scratchity voice from across the lawn interrupted Arley's complaining. *Who is that old guy growling at Dad?* Arley wondered.

"So…just a warnin', Mr. Ketring: People in the neighborhood say basements stay dry 'nuff, but the cement blocks down there may be a-crumplin'. Better keep those kids o' yors away from the blocks." The man had to be 100 years old shaking a bony finger in Dad's face. Short and bent at several angles, he still looked strong. He wore old farming clothes and the guy's head…well, Arley's been taught to respect older (and even odder) people, but the guy's head made Arley grin. Hair hung in grey strings around his face. The very top of the guy's head was bald and brown as a football but not as smooth.

Dad was assuring the old guy, "OK, Mr. Harold. I'll check on the basement blocks as soon as we get settled. Thanks for stopping by. Now, where do you live?"

"Oh, just around…And, one more thing, young man…" At this Arley chuckled out loud. *My dad, a young man? Hardly! Dad's at least in his 40s!*

"…lights flicker a lot in this neighborhood," Mr. Harold went on. "Pay no mind."

"That's odd!" Dad sounded surprised. "Neither the seller nor the bank mentioned anything about…"

"Hmph!" Mr. Harold grunted and turned away from

Dad. The old man turned squinty eyes on Arley as they passed; then, Mr. Harold gave Arley a curling mouth. He hobbled down the driveway.

Arley noticed ol' Mr. Harold had a light bulb sticking out of his back pocket. *Creepy! I guess Mr. Harold keeps one of those just in case his own lights flicker,* Arley joked to himself, appreciating the pun. But in a second, Arley felt a tug of guilt.

∽∽∽

Four weeks of junior high were not proving kind to Arley; neither was the move from the Ketring's old country house to this two-story brick in town. "No woods or caves to explore around here," groused Arley at the dinner table, stabbing at his potatoes and chicken in disappointed rebellion. "No corn fields, no streams, no horses or chickens allowed in town. And who do we have for next door neighbors? Dead People!!"

"Arley Ketring!" Mom said with a gasp. "The funeral home is a most respectable business! And…if you think about it, at least those neighbors are quiet!" Mom grinned and squeezed Arley's arm. She cleared her throat and then coughed a bit. She excused herself quickly to get her medicine.

Dad was willing to explain again, but felt irritation rising inside himself. He wondered why the numerous family discussions about this new home purchase, along with discussions for months before the family actually moved, had not impressed his son. "Arley!" Dad said the boy's name a bit too firmly. Dad stopped and took a calming breath. "Son, we now have close neighbors…other LIVING neighbors."

Here, Dad paused and stared at Arley for effect. "…neighbors who will become friends and can help us on days Mom gets sick. Remember, we talked about fewer driving expenses and less property upkeep. Consider your freedoms, Son: you can walk to school, the bike park, the dog park, and even to church youth group and some school activities. No more worry about missing out on things you want to do because of no transportation! This move is good for our whole family." And then Dad chided, "You should be grateful, Arley…"

"Yeah, Dad. **I'M** grateful," interrupted eight-year-old Ryder. "Here in town I like to walk Sasha around the block and…" Ryder stopped suddenly when he saw Arley glaring at him.

Ryder's red hair fell over his eyes and his cheeks burned. He studied his own mashed potatoes. Ryder certainly admired his big brother but feared his wrath. A big brother could make life miserable for a little kid.

I used to like this kid, Arley thought, finishing his food glumly, *like when he was a baby or a tot. But now?* Arley thought Ryder was always getting into his stuff and following him around too much. Arley especially hated it when Ryder butted in on serious adult conversations Arley would have with Mom and Dad. *The kid always comes off with that red-headed cuteness!* Arley grimaced. *He's a dork! I have a dork for a brother!*

Mom returned to the table and reached out for Arley's hand, "When you're done eating, honey, will you please run to the basement…" the lights in the house suddenly flickered. But it was just an instantaneous off-on. Everyone stopped mid-bite and looked up at the ceiling light. "…Oh!" Mom shrugged and everyone went right back to their meal. "Anyway, Arley, please put the washed laundry into the dryer, will you? Then, bring your homework to the den. We'll knock out tomorrow's school assignments together."

Twelve minutes later the laundry was still on the final spin cycle, so Arley kicked around the basement, looking for those "crumplin" cement blocks ol' Mr. Harold had warned Dad about.

"More than 'crumplin'," said Arley aloud. "Look at this one block nearly falling out of the mortar!" He tried to push it back in place, but the mortar crumbled even faster. The heavy block was now leaning out of its place balanced in Arley's hands.

"Whoa," Arley whispered and noted the washer had stopped spinning. Arley shoved the block into the hole sideways. Turning toward the laundry corner, his peripheral sight grabbed a pinhead of light from the blackness behind the block. "Whaaat…?"

"Arley? Coming?" called Mom, which started her coughing fit.

"Yeah, sorry, Mom. Be right there." Arley switched the laundry. He slapped the dryer button on high and bolted up the steps.

ꜩꜩꜩ

It wasn't the best time for Dad to leave on a business trip. By mid-October, the Ketring family was still unpacking and remodeling a couple rooms; Arley needed his dad's help with math every evening, and, of course, the autumn was never a good time for Mom to be alone. Chilly weather only incensed[†] her congestion.

"It will be less than a week, honey," Dad told Mom with

a kiss. He pointed his finger at his boys with a smile as if to say, "Take care of her!" Arley knew what that meant: extra chores and extra allowance! The young teen spent the entire Thursday evening after Dad left actually looking for chores. But Ryder spent the same time refusing to acknowledge any such thing as chores. Arley wondered briefly if he could try to fix the busted block in the basement, but he didn't know the first thing about masonry[†] work.

Friday evening Mom sat on the porch swing with Sasha at her feet. Sasha was a beautiful grey standard poodle. She was not only the family's fuzzy and funny pet, but also she was Mom's service dog.[†] Sasha loyally protected Mom and often predicted Mom's congestion emergencies. This evening, Mom was wearing a cough mask over her mouth and nose due to the sudden chill after a balmy day. But she was toasty, zipped up in Dad's hoodie. Arley stepped out onto the porch and dug his fingers into Sasha's woolly coat. "Mom, can I go…" he started to ask.

"I wanna go, too!" Ryder appeared out of nowhere and was shouting and clapping his hands. Arley rolled his eyes and wished the kid would go back where he came from. *Ha, nowhere!* Arley chuckled to himself.

Mom's look silenced Ryder. Without turning her stare from Ryder's face, she said calmly to Arley, "Were you trying to say something, Arley?" The teen turned his back to Kid Brother and bent to whisper to Mom, "Yeah, thanks, Mom. Homecoming Game tonight, just a 20-minute walk."

"Me too, me too!" Ryder was now hopping around in excitement.

"You don't even know where…" Arley spit out at Ryder.

"Yes, Arley, go ahead to the game," Mom interrupted the

boiling argument. *My mom, always playing the referee,* thought Arley with an expanded heart.[†] Mom continued, "Ryder can stay and help me pour coffee for my three friends stopping by."

Arley wanted to turn and stick out his tongue at Kid Brother, but then he remembered, in horror, the one time **he** had had to stay home to help out during his mom's coffee klatch.[†] It had to be **theee one** most boring and ridiculous time in Arley's 13 years. He remembered: *those silly tiny cups of coffee, those even-tinier cookies with colored candy sprinkles, the laughing ladies, and poor Sasha reduced to begging, literally, for crumbs!* Almost in a panic for his brother, Arley blurted out, "Oh no! I mean, well, if it's OK, Mom, I guess Ryder can tag along with me." And then, Arley wondered in a daze, *What did I just say?*

Mom raised her eyebrows until they nearly met her hairline, "Wel...well, OK then," Mom stuttered, her eyes wide and grinning from ear to ear. Ryder began a screeching Indian dance. "Keep him close, Arley," Mom advised.

"OK. Let's get ready, Red, " Arley said as he warmed to the idea. He suddenly remembered how much the girls at the new school liked this cute little red-headed brother!

After a chilly evening and a hard-fought battle on the football field, the hometown won. The two brothers walked home ten feet apart, both dreamy-eyed and smiling at their own thoughts: Ryder, because he was sure his whooping, hollering, and cheering helped the home team get their sixth and then the seventh winning touchdowns. Arley? He was smiling because two cheerleaders came by after the game to talk to him. No matter it was Ryder to whom they waved throughout the entire evening and stopped by to meet. Ryder had basically ignored the girls, but Arley charmed them with his tales of boarding and breaking horses,[†] "...at our old place in the country."

When the boys hit the porch, Mom was already in bed...coughing. They refilled her water bottle and plumped the pillows. "I'm not sure I can manage the steps to the basement, boys. Will you take over the laundry chore until Dad returns in a few more days?"

"Sure, Mom," Ryder started as he sat on Mom's bed.

"Ryder, you don't even know which is the washer and which is the dryer," Arley bit, but then softened, "Yeah, we'll do it, Mom."

Mom took a long drink and whispered, "Maybe it's time for Ryder to learn which machine is which and how to sort clothes and how much detergent to use...just like you learned, Arley. You're a really good big brother, and I bet a great teacher, too."

"OK, Mom. I'll show him the tricks of the trade. Love you," Arley kissed Mom's forehead and the boys left her room.

ﻮﻮﻮ

Late that Friday night, Ryder jumped into his Pokemon pajamas. Yawning, he crawled under his bed quilt to play his game piece. Mom had been asleep for about an hour. Arley was grazing from the fridge when the lights flickered, then went off. He pulled his head out of the dark fridge and blinked. The kitchen was black, as well. *Oh, no! I hope I don't have to replace a light bulb!* Arley fretted. Just as suddenly, the lights flashed back on in the kitchen and inside the fridge. Arley grabbed a slice of cold pizza and headed down the basement steps. He knelt down at the busted block and peeked behind it. There was still a sea of darkness but with that same dot of light far away. *Wow! Where is that coming from? And, shouldn't there be a solid dirt wall behind these blocks?* Arley wondered.

He found the big bulky orange flashlight and pointed it into the space left by the sideways block. There were stringy cobwebs and little piles of crumbled mortar. But very far away, there still shone a pinpoint of silvery light. Arley guessed, *Looks like it could be as far away as the funeral home,* which sat at the south side of the empty lot next door. "That is creepy," he said aloud.

ZING! A bead of something ricocheted off his flashlight. BOP! Something fell into his hair. Then, Arley grabbed his hand, "OUCH!" Something pointy had struck and stung the back of his hand. He looked up to see vibrating mortar all around several cement blocks immediately above this busted one. One by one tiny and then larger chunks of mortar spit out of their places and began to rain down on Arley. The blocks themselves were shimmying and threatening a collapse of the entire wall. Arley jumped off his knees and backwards, shocked at the show.

"So, I beat it outta there," Arley whispered to Ryder over breakfast the next morning. "I didn't hear any crashes overnight, so I guess the vibrations stopped. Wonder what that tiny light could be...And DON'T YOU tell Mom ANY of this 'til we figure it all out." The boys told Mom they were going to unpack boxes and do laundry in the basement for most of their Saturday. When they scuttled down the steps, the cement blocks were too heavy for Ryder to lift, but he could "roll" them to a corner. Arley did the heavy work of part-pulling and part-dropping the blocks to the floor. Arley's face was sweating all around his goggles after he removed four blocks. That left an opening in the wall that the boys could crawl into and enter single-file.

"Definitely a tunnel," said Arley. "Do you see that point of light?"

"Maybe it's the sun shining into a hole in the ground?" said Ryder, feeling grown up to be in on Arley's secret adventure.

"How does the sun shine into a tunnel underground?" Arley was already exasperated with an eight-year-old's thinking process. "That can't be…I bet this tunnel hooks to another tunnel going to the funeral home where the light starts," guessed Arley. Then, he crawled into the mouth of the tunnel and belted out an excited, "Let's go!"

"W-w-wait, Arley. Maybe I oughta check on Mom first." Ryder wasn't keen on the idea of crawling toward the funeral home. *Dead bodies!* Ryder wondered if there might be bodies or skeletons scattered in the tunnel, too. But he saw Arley's rear end wiggling away into the dark and his little boy's sense of adventure kicked in. "Hey! Here I come!"

Sasha barked as Mom answered the door, "Good morning, may I help…" Mom was interrupted by a scratchity voice from a bent old man at her door.

"Did the Mr. fix the loose blocks yet?"

"What? Who are yo…"

"Oh sorry, I'm Mr. Harold, are you Mrs. Ketring?" But without waiting for an answer, the old bent man hurried on, "I talked to your husband, warned 'im about the crumplin' blocks in the basement."

"Uhh, blocks? Basement? I don't know anything about…"

"Is he around?" blurted Mr. Harold, straining to look over Mom's shoulder, his manner all brusque and business.

"Well, not at the moment…can I have him call you?" Mom asked, rising up to Mr. Harold's impertinence.[†] She felt a slight nervous constriction of her airways and covered a cough. Then, Sasha growled softly, deep in her throat.

"OK, just don't let dem kids o' yours play around the loose blocks," Mr. Harold ordered.

"Where exactly are…"

But Mr. Harold had already turned away and was gimping down the driveway. He bent in half to peek into a basement window. Sasha barked. Mr. Harold straightened quickly and threw a menacing look toward Sasha. He hurried away.

"Boys!" Mom called down the steps, feeling growing anxiety. Sasha sniffed the air and barked once at the top of the stairs. "Boys, what are you doing down there? Boys! Are you doing laundry?" Mom's voice was strained at her increased volume. Sasha pointed her snout at the funeral home. She sniffed the floor and whined. She turned a circle and whined again.

"What is it, Girl?" Mom reached for the dog's head but Sasha ran. She sniffed the floor; she sniffed her way through the kitchen, down the hall and into the far south bedroom. When Mom caught up with Sasha, she began to wheeze. Mom caught the door jam and purposefully slowed her breath. She took a long draw on her water bottle. Sasha continued to growl and whine sorely. Mom lifted her eyes to the window. She started; her hand flew to her chest.

At the edge of the empty lot between her new home and the funeral home, Mom saw the man who was just at her door. *Harold, was that his name?* Mom wondered. The old man was holding up something long and shiny. It seemed to be a six-foot thin pole of some sort, more like a spear. Mr. Harold was jabbing the sharp arrow head into the ground, over and over and over again.

; ; ;

"Gettin' chilly," complained Kid Brother, crawling slowly behind Arley.

Why did I bring him in on this adventure? Arley scolded himself. They were close enough now to note that the tiny dot of light was really a bare light bulb shining thinly. It was hanging on a black braided electric cord.

"Just ten more minutes, Kid," encouraged Arley over his shoulder. They began to hear a TAP-TAPPING. "Hear that? Maybe comin' from the light bulb room?"

Suddenly, a SLASH through the air by Arley's head brought dirt flying into his eyes. He scrambled backwards and squeezed his eyes open and shut. He saw a spear head disappear upwards and another come down and SLAM into a rock beside Ryder's hand.

"GO BACK, G'BACK, G'BACK, G'BACK," screamed Arley. The boys whipped around and sped back toward their basement, scraping foreheads, knees, elbows, and palms.

They heard another SLICE behind them but closer to the light bulb. They heard another and another and another. The slices into the earth began to sound fainter, and the dust wasn't flying around them any longer. Arley looked back and saw the spear head still crashing all around the light bulb. But the danger seemed to be behind them now.

"Slow down," Arley called. Ryder looked back with dirty tear tracks down his face and crusty snot under his nose. The boys huddled together, exhausted, breathing dust, gagging and spitting. They looked toward the light bulb which was, once again, a tiny shiny dot. But the light seemed to be blinking. Arley knew, however, that the spear was still at work, cutting off their line of sight to the light, slice-by-slice-by-slice.

The boys crept, as in a daze, toward their basement.

What just happened? Arley wondered. Soon the boys heard a muffled Sasha barking and Mom calling. As they crawled closer still, Arley knew Mom was coughing…and crying, as well.

පපප

It was Saturday noon when the battle-broken[†] boys finished telling Mom the whole story. She simply arose and called the police. The department sent two blue-and-green cruisers, with lights flashing, to the Ketring family home. While police took an official statement from the boys, a social worker comforted Mom. The initial police investigation found the lacerated earth on the empty lot next door. Official yellow police tape went up, but the detectives had to locate the landowner before they could move forward on the investigation.

Mom and the boys double-locked all the doors and windows. Sasha sniffed the boys and then the perimeter of the house. Mom made hot cocoa and sandwiches while the boys took turns showering. They all sat together in warm PJs, all afternoon, stunned. They did not want to talk about this frightening mystery, but were unable to speak of anything else. Sasha ambled aimlessly about the house and softly whined for the rest of the day. She circled and laid her head in Mom's lap every hour.

Despite half-hearted attempts at homework, table games, and a movie, all four were asleep by early Saturday evening. Dad finally arrived late in the night. Mom awoke and told him all the details. The boys and Sasha snored loudly. Dad checked the basement and found the dislodged and broken blocks, but he found no tunnel. He stabbed at the dirt wall, but it was solid. "There's no tunnel! What happened here?" he whispered.

On Sunday afternoon the family met the estate guardian, Mr. Chad Harold Higgins. He was the great-nephew of the deceased owner, Mr. Jonathan Harold. Mr. Chad had given the city permission to dig around the area. Investigators could not determine what tool…or weapon had been used to disturb the ground. However, no electricity was found on that side of the property, and they uncovered no light bulb on a braided cord. Neither was a tunnel found.

Mr. Chad Harold Higgins sympathized with Dad and the boys, all gathered at the sliced-and-diced spot… "but, as I told the police earlier, my great-uncle died two years ago. I cannot think of anyone who'd visit you, impersonating Great-Uncle John. You are quite sure this old man said his name was, 'Mr. Harold?'"

"Yes, I'm sure," said Dad. "He introduced himself to me. My son, Arley, overheard him talking to me the very morning we moved in. This 'Mr. Harold' even warned us about the 'crumplin', I mean the crumbling blocks in the basement. And, he tried to scare my wife…" Dad was getting irritated with thin explanations.

"Well…I don't know, sir!" Chad Higgins interrupted Dad to allow him to calm down. Chad looked at Arley and scratched his own prematurely balding head, "This is such a crazy thing! However, Arley, your physical description of Great-Uncle John is spot on! The football head, the stringy grey hair, his pointy bent elbows and knees…Amazing!" Arley blushed at hearing his unflattering description of Mr. Harold spoken aloud.

Tired and frustrated, Arley walked home to tell Mom the latest news, which was no news. Dad and Great-Nephew Chad went to the sheriff's cruiser to look at police photos of older miscreants[†] in the area. Ryder hovered around the cruiser trying to take in the mystery. Of course, so much of life is mysterious to an eight-year-old. He still imagined that the tunnel's pinpoint of light was just sunshine squeezing into the earth through holes in the dirt. And, Ryder thought Mr. Harold must be a ghost. *He probably lives right there at the funeral home.* Ryder shivered and off went his imagination.

"Hellooooo! Come here, boy!"

Ryder noticed an old lady at the funeral home side door waving her hankie and squeaking out, "Youuuuuu-hooooo! Boyeee! Come here!" Ryder wondered if she was calling a dog, but when he lifted his face toward her, she pointed a long bony finger right at him, "You, boy. Please come here!"

"Dad, that lady…"

"Yes, I heard her too, Ryder," Dad said. "Run over and see what she wants."

Dad returned to the last screen of mug shots, but none had matched the family's remembrance of the supposed "Mr. Harold."

Great-Nephew Chad was stumped. He pulled at his chin, "Y'know, I can't imagine that anyone who knew Uncle John would think he would chop up the ground like that! He owned the property here beside the funeral home for 72 years. He never had a house on it. He never grew any crops or gardens here, never grazed animals…yet, Great-Uncle John would never let us dispose of it."

"Maybe sentiment[†]?" Dad asked.

"Well, he was raised in the funeral home here which

his parents owned—that would beeee, let's seeeee..." At this, Chad raised his eyes to the sky and pulled at his chin. "Ah, yes, Uncle John's dad would be my great-granddad. He first owned this funeral home. I never really knew Great-Uncle John well. I cannot imagine what attachment he had to this property," Chad concluded.

∽∽∽

The following week the investigation dragged on, but the Ketring family was not privy to official information. While Dad and the boys worked on repairing the cement blocks in the basement, Dad sighed, "Boys, I know we've already beat this dead horse, but look once again. Look behind these broken blocks. Do you see a tunnel?"

Ryder slowly put up his hand, as if he were in his second-grade classroom, his face long and droopy under his shock of red hair. Dad turned and grinned at the sweet and absurd sight.

"Yes, Ryder, do you have a question?" Dad asked while Arley rolled his eyes.

"Well, yeah. Like...well, when did someone kill a horse down here, Dad? And is that maybe why Mr. Harold came back to haunt us?" Ryder had a tear brimming in the corner of one eye.

"Oh, my goodness!" Arley breathed out with a little venom.

"Arley, it's alright," said Dad patting Arley's shoulder to stop the scorn. Dad pulled Ryder onto his lap as he slouched in his sports chair. "Ryder, 'beating a dead horse,' is an expression for...Wait! Maybe Arley can tell us..." Dad raised his eyebrows and looked into his teenager's eyes, as a challenge. Arley's cheeks burned. Then, composing himself, "...OK, well, 'beating a dead horse' is an expression[†] for talking and talking and talking about something that hasn't been solved by talking...and probably won't be solved by talking."

"Bravo, Son!" beamed Dad.

Ryder understood, sort of, but he was eager to keep beating the horse (talking about this conundrum[†]). "I know, Dad, it's only a dirt wall where these cement blocks should be, but it **IS** indented deeper than the blocks, right? And, maybe Mr. Harold's ghost filled in the tunnel with dirt and..."

Dad held up his hand to stop Ryder's babbling and looked at Arley for his ideas of what may have happened. "I-I-I just don't know, Dad. You can't believe that Ryder and I dreamed all this up! Do you? You and Mom met Mr. Harold, too, so not everything can be explained as our fantasy... and the chopped up ground...and our bruised hands and knees from crawling and, and..." Arley wasn't scared by this mystery like Ryder was, but was more than frustrated. "Let's just get back to work," Arley shrugged and turned away. He wouldn't let Dad see his tears.

By the beginning of November Chad Harold Higgins asked the city to dismiss the investigation of trespassing and vandalism on the property between the Ketring home and the funeral home. Chad reasoned with the Police Department, "There is no obvious trespasser and little damage was done. The only lead we have to investigate is my great-uncle,

Jonathan Harold, who is deceased. And, if you think about it," joked Chad, "the property is his, to do with as he likes anyway!"

"Cavalier,[†] Mr. Higgins," noted the police chief. "Yes, with your signature we can close the Ketring-Higgins case. Please let us know if we can help in any other civil or criminal matter."

It was early Christmas Season before the mystery demanded the Ketring family's attention again. Mom had become ill and spent Thanksgiving week in the hospital. The whole family was focused on caring for her, besides the boys' regular school work and Dad's business. One evening Sasha began barking at the top of the basement stairs. "Quiet, Girl! Mom's sleeping," whispered Arley. Sasha barked again. "Sasha! I said, quiet…oh, I see what you are telling me, Girl. The basement light is still on. Good, Girl." Arley scruffed Sasha's head and walked to the top of the stairs to flip the light switch off, but the light didn't go off. He flipped the switch up and down, up and down, but the light stayed the same. *What is it with these crazy flickering lights?* Arley wondered.

He squatted at the top of the steps and noticed the basement window was full of bright light. Curious, he jumped down the steps two at a time and stretched up to look out the high basement window.

Whoa! He breathed. Arley saw the light coming from the beautiful Christmas décor on the front pillars of the funeral home. It seemed to fill the basement and the whole neighborhood with a shimmering brightness. A perfect Christmas scene! *Oh, holy night!* He thought.

There were huge silver wreaths hanging on each of the four pillars at the front porch of the funeral home. The wreaths were made of silvery paper shreds like thin strips of aluminum foil. When the slightest breeze blew, each little paper sliver wiggled around and reflected all kinds of light beams. Flashes were scattering from the wreaths and reflecting off the snow. Arley noticed a candle flame in the middle of each wreath. *No, wait! Not a candle...* Arley thought as he squinted his eyes. He focused on one wreath, then the second wreath, then the third and fourth, one-by-one. With wide and unbelieving eyes he saw in the middle of each silver wreath there hung a single bare light bulb...each hanging from a black braided electric cord.

∽∽∽

"Christmas Eve Day," Mom sighed. The family was eating their breakfast at 7 a.m. They had a busy agenda for this holiday. Mom continued, "What a sad time of the year for a family to have to face a funeral." The family looked out the window to see the parking lot at the funeral home filling up for a morning visitation.

"Christmas Eve! A funeral!" Ryder shouted and jumped up from the table. "That's it!" Mom was startled. Sasha barked. Lights flickered.

"Quiet down!" bossed Arley.

"What do you mean, Ryder?" Dad asked.

"The...that lady who lives in the back apartment at the funeral home—she dusts and vacuums for the place—she said a Christmas Eve funeral would solve our mystery...a-a-a-about the tunnel and the chopped ground a-a-and...." Ryder was stuttering, gesturing, and walking in a dazed circle.

"What? Slow down. When did you talk to that la..." Dad started. "Oh, yes! The one who called you over when we were talking to the police? You never told us what she said, Ryder."

"Guess I forgot. I was going to tell you while we fixed the busted blocks but that dead horse business scared it right out of me. Anyway, she said that there would be a funeral on Christmas Eve Day—that's today! And then, she said, we would meet Mr. Harold."

"What?! What are you talkin'...? Really? What?" Arley was mad. "How can you forget something like that, Ryder? What is wrong with you?"

However, Arley had a secret of his own. He had not told his family about the naked light bulbs in the wreaths next door. No one in the family had mentioned the Christmas decorations at the funeral home. Even if Mom or Dad had noticed the braided cord with a naked hanging light bulb, it may have meant nothing to them. Only Ryder and Arley saw the bulb on the black cord hanging in the tunnel. Anyway, the whole family was still shaken by the mystery they could not solve; but no one talked about it.

Dad stood suddenly and ordered, "Boys, come to the basement with me." He was ready to reopen the subject once again, but not within Mom's hearing.

In the basement Ryder simply repeated what he had said upstairs because he couldn't remember any more. And, he felt guilty for not telling his family this news earlier.

"Well, would you look at that!" Arley tried to sound nonchalant, as if he himself were just discovering the wreaths and light bulbs next door. He pointed out the window, across the vacant property to the front of the funeral home. Dad failed to see the significance and wanted to get the boys back on track with the discussion. However, Ryder had stepped up a short ladder to look out the window. He looked, shrugged and looked at Arley. Arley's eyes were huge and menacing; he jerked his head toward the funeral home as if to say, "look again!" Ryder did…and then, he began to cry in fear.

Suddenly, a few tiny pieces of mortar began to chip and spit out from between the cement blocks…from the very same place Dad and the boys had repaired. Dad pushed his big hands against the blocks and felt vibrations. His eyes seemed to bulge and his mouth fell open. Larger chunks of mortar cracked and fell to the basement floor. Arley grabbed Ryder and backed up to the steps. "Dad, let's get out of here," Arley demanded. Ryder just cried harder.

As suddenly as it began, the trembling wall stopped. No one breathed. There was a grating sound like dragging your bicycle on its side, the pedal grinding all the way down the driveway. Two concrete blocks shimmied into Dad's strong arms. He jumped back and dropped them to the floor. From across the basement, the boys saw it right away. A great black hole and a faraway pinpoint of light! Dad looked in. "A tunnel," he whispered.

Then, everything seemed to move in slow motion. As Dad turned toward the boys, Arley thought he noticed every thread in Dad's shirt and every hair on his head. Dad's face was white and his eyes, huge and wet. Dad, in shock, longed for his boys and simply held out his arms. The boys stepped into his embrace and all three stuck their heads into the tunnel.

The police and fire fighters investigated the tunnel from the Ketring family basement. By 9 a.m. Dad took Mom, the boys, and Sasha to the pastor's house for safekeeping. It was late morning, Christmas Eve morning, when the investigators learned that the funeral next door was for one of Mr. Chad Harold Higgins' relatives. A detective was assigned to meet with Chad and find the cleaning lady. During the last few minutes of the funeral visitation, Detective Angela Sal briefed the funeral home directors about her visit "...for official business," she said. However, she did not mention her plan to interview the cleaning lady in the back apartment later. Sal had been involved in the Ketring-Higgins incident from the beginning, but only from her desk. She had read all the reports and saw all the pictures. Oh! How she loved a mystery! How would they connect this Christmas Eve funeral, the appearances of the suspected-but-dead "Mr. Harold," the tunnel and the funeral home's wreaths with bare light bulbs on braided electrical cords?

Sal pulled the photo of the cleaning lady that the funeral home had provided out of her uniform pocket. It was eerily similar to an old photo, provided by Great-Nephew Chad Harold Higgins, of the late Mr. Jonathan Harold. Sal, young and on her first detective assignment, wondered, *Do all elderly, deceased people groomed for their funerals end up looking alike? Or maybe just people associated with this funeral home look alike?* She shivered at the creepy photos.

Detective Sal was escorted to the casket and to meet the family. She was greeted by the unsuspecting Chad Harold Higgins whom she had never met. "Thank you for coming, Detective. How did you know my grandmother?" Chad welcomed the supposed-mourner. Sal began to offer condolences and explain that this was an official visit. But as she glanced at the deceased in the open casket, she stopped dead. Chad's grandmother, Mrs. Beverly Harold Higgins, looked exactly like Sal's photo of the cleaning lady! And so similar to her photo of the late Mr. Jonathan Harold.

∽∽∽

At the Christmas Eve afternoon bereavement dinner,[†] Detective Sal interviewed Chad. "I'll start, sir, if you don't mind," suggested Sal.

"Please," Chad opened his palm to accept her questions.

"Why didn't you tell us that your grandmother was the

deceased Jonathan Harold's twin sister...AND the cleaning lady for the funeral home?"

"Didn't think of it, Detective. Sincerely, I never thought I could involve her in the investigation. The funeral home told me that she was nearly bedfast for months and that dementia[†] had dulled her thinking and speech. I'm ashamed to admit that I didn't visit her much and I knew very little about her life...until this week."

"The PD just learned today that your grandmother... or that is, some older lady who introduced herself as the cleaning lady here, spoke to the little Ketring boy on the very day that the family reported the sighting of the slice-dice incident."

"I'm struggling with so many things I've learned in just the last few hours, Detective." Chad looked dazed.

"Sooo..." Detective Sal stalled for Chad to go on, but he didn't offer anything. "So, it seems your grandmother predicted her own funeral on Christmas Eve! And, she promised a solved mystery regarding Mr. Harold. What do you make of that?"

"I'm sorry that I cannot solve everything about this mystery, Detective." Chad spoke slowly, but looked as if light bulbs were shining in his eyes. "Grandma and Uncle John," Chad's voice trailed off. He looked away; he seemed to be pondering.

"Chad? Uh, Mr. Higgins, please focus. Can you help us solve this mystery?"

"Oh, yes, ma'am, I'm sorry." Chad Harold Higgins began to explain, "A few family members took turns staying with Grandma this past week, as she was failing. Grandma Beverly always chattered about nonsensical family stories.

She was a rambler, if you will, in her conversation. Last week, she talked about playing hide-and-seek, dark tunnels, and naked light bulbs. We never knew what to believe, so we just let her talk. We really paid little attention."

"As far as you know, has she ever alluded to this tunnel story before in her life, Chad?" asked Sal.

"Oh, no. This seemed to be a deeply buried family secret...no pun intended," chuckled Chad, chugging his strong black coffee. "But during her last couple days, her stories made her cry. Although sad, she was lucid[†] in her thoughts and sentences. She described how she and her twin brother, Great-Uncle John, used to hide in the tunnels from their dad. That would be my great-grandfather. He was the original owner of this funeral home. Other relatives have insinuated[†] over the years that Great-Grandpa was alcoholic and vicious. But no family member ever shared details or actual events.

"Why tunnels?" asked Sal.

"Well, Grandma said that when the pair were just seven years old, Uncle John dug a little hidden basement hole for them to jump into whenever their dad came home drunk. Grandma said that as John grew bigger and stronger, he dug numerous tunnels where they could be safe. They explored and played in the tunnels for hours at a time...usually on weekends after their dad got paid. That's when Great-Grandpa drank the most...Grandma said." Chad looked like he was watching an old family movie, even as he told the story. He had tears in his eyes. "As you can tell, what I am repeating is pretty clear and sensible, sensitive and personal information that Grandma poured out on us." His voice caught.

"Was there a mother around for the kids?" asked Sal gently.

"Well, yes…I never knew her, of course. I'm told she died in childbirth while delivering another baby who didn't live. Some family members wonder if Great-Grandpa was as mean to his wife as Grandma Beverly reported he was to John and herself.

"Anyway, Grandma's dad never found the tunnels and Grandma and Uncle John 'guarded their hide-away with their lives,' is the way Grandma said it. She told us Uncle John was her savior, always protecting her." Chad stood to take a deep breath, then excused himself to the restroom. On his way out of the room, Chad checked the light bulbs in two sofa lamps, turned them on and off and back on, again off, on, off.

෴෴෴

"Technical question, Mr. Higgins?" asked Sal when Chad returned. She would attempt to steer clear of emotional questions and pull out the facts.

"Shoot, Ms. Sal."

"How do you suppose the children ran electricity…for the light bulbs, that is?"

"Oh! That's easy. I don't think they had lights at all when they were young. Grandma talked about the dark hours they spent running through the tunnels. She was often frightened of the dark, of course. And, she DID say they occasionally heard 'little landslides' in the tunnels. They could not have been expertly packed tunnels, obviously. Perhaps the vibrations over the years, from modern traffic and heavy household appliances, have made the hollowed out tunnels susceptible to imploding.[†] I think that's why the police didn't find the tunnel in the empty lot back in October. We may never find all the tunnels."

"Annnnnd sooooo, back to the topic of the lights?" Sal prompted.

"Oh, yeah…Well, what do you think of this? Perhaps, when they were adults, maybe even just teens, the twins ran electricity to create a shrine for their childhood, their underground life. If that's the case, it makes sense to me why Uncle John refused to let go of this property."

"So, we both know that your great-uncle Jonathan Harold, two years deceased, did not haunt the Ketring family or chop up the ground over the tunnel the boys were exploring," suggested Sal, trying to tie up the biggest mystery of all—the "whodunit.[†]"

"Let me show you something, Detective." Chad opened a bag under the table. He pulled out some very old farmer's clothes and a wig. "These were among Grandma's personal effects and they both have recently been worn. These are Uncle John's old clothes, the very clothes the Ketring family recognized when I visited them this morning. And look at this bald wig with stringy hair, also identified by Arley as 'Mr. Harold's' head."

"Wait. What?" Sal's eyes bulged. "You talked to the Ketrings? Today?"

"Oh, yes. I went immediately when I saw the fire trucks and police. I was worried about them."

"But, but, you discussed this case with them?" Sal stuttered. She could hardly believe that Chad and the Ketrings had already convened[†] their own little investigation, of sorts…without her!

"Well, Detective, this isn't really a case yet. Have the Ketrings made any charges?"

Sal was stunned. She was slow to recover. She closed her notebook. She asked for a cup of coffee. When Chad returned to the table, he patted Sal's shoulder. She sipped the steaming brew. "So, here's what we believe happened back in October, Detective." Chad began, "Grandma Beverly used her very last bit of strength to disguise herself as her twin brother and protect their life-long secret. I don't think Grandma Beverly was as bedfast as the funeral director thought.

"And, here's something else, I learned: Grandma often carried and hid bare light bulbs in 'places a sundry.'[†] Perhaps her dark childhood had so unsettled her…? This is all quite weird, I know, very weird. But to my great-uncle and grandma, their tunnel life was a precious secret to which they were completely loyal."

"Would you be willing, sir, for me to jot a few notes from our discussion into the October case as an end to this matter?" Sal's head was spinning, but as a professional, she was ready to take her leave. It was Christmas Eve, after all.

"Oh, of course. And, if you will excuse me, I must get back to my family. Grandma Beverly's funeral is in an hour. Call me, Detective, when I can review your final report." After a handshake with Sal, Chad stepped away from the table. Sal began to gather her notebook and bag when she noticed Chad on his way out. He quickly reached into a planter boasting large and drooping ferns. He pulled out a bare light bulb and stuck it in his suit pocket.

"Yep, weird," Sal mumbled.

❧❧❧

"Thanks so much, Pastor, for keeping us all day. I think we've all had enough excitement. We are eager for a very quiet Christmas Eve," Dad grabbed the pastor's hand for a strong shake.

"Alex Ketring, don't you ever worry that you have imposed on us. May God bless your family and Merry Christmas!" The pastor clapped Dad on the back.

Mom fell asleep immediately in the car, and Sasha stretched out between the boys in the back seat. "Dad, what do you think of Mr. Chad's invitation to Ryder and me to help him hunt for tunnels?"

"Well, Son, he did say 'next summer,' and there's a lot of time between now and then."

Yeah, but it does sound pretty cool, doesn't it? I mean, walking all over that empty lot pushing the GPR machine (ground-penetrating radar),[†] hunting for his Uncle John's tunnels?"

"I don't know how ground-penetrating radar works exactly, Arley. I think it would be a fun explore for both of you boys. I wouldn't mind checking out the machine myself."

"What do you think he'd do if he does find a lot of tunnels?"

"Well, Arley, he cannot sell the property until he knows what is underground…or not. If anyone bought the property and tried to build and found numerous caves or tunnels, machinery could wreck, people could get hurt, and…well, it could be bad."

"So, is that a 'yes,' Dad? Can we spend next summer with Chad hunting for tunnels?" Arley pushed.

"I'm thinking only one thing right now, Arley, and I won't change my mind." Dad paused and grinned. After a

full minute, Arley leaned up over the back of Mom's seat, staring at his dad's profile.

"Welllll…Dad? What's the one thing you are thinking?"

"Merry Christmas, Son." Dad reached over to rub Arley's head. "A very Merry Christmas!" Arley grinned, yawned, and fell back to his seat. He looked out the window to gaze at all the Christmas lights.

Glossary and Story Questions

Professional incompetence Professionals must gain certain skills or understanding to continue successfully in their chosen or awarded discipline. They should abide by certain high standards of conduct because they often deal with the general public and must advocate for the welfare of others. The word 'incompetence' is usually identified with people without such skill, understanding, or tools and therefore, people who do not attain to business or relationship success. The two words should not "fit" together or be used together because they should never present a true picture of any situation or person.

However, when two opposite-meaning words **are** used together to make a phrase and they **do** present a true picture of the situation or person, this is called an oxymoron. Generally, an oxymoron triggers frustration for people who understand the oxymoron… like Arley's Dad's frustration over professional incompetence!

Look up the word "oxymoron" and write down three of them here:

Incensed means very angry, enraged; in this case, the weather irritated Mom's breathing until her respiratory system reacted like an angry thing—coughing, gagging, difficulty breathing.

Masonry is repair or building work using stone, brick, concrete, etc. The person who does such work is called a mason.

Service Dog a type of assistance dog (or perhaps other animals) trained to help people who have disabilities or some other companion need, i.e., visual or hearing impairments, seizure disorders, hospice, etc.

Research to answer the following interesting questions regarding service dogs:

- What types/breeds of dogs are best suited to become service dogs?
- What disabilities may dogs be trained to service?
- What kind of training must dogs receive to become service dogs?
- What qualifies a person to receive a service dog?
- What might it cost to own a service dog?
- What questions might you add to this list?

Expanded Heart In this case, Arley's heart (his feelings) expanded or grew larger or warmer from being angry and shut off from his brother (our hearts feel small and hard and tight when we are angry) to suddenly feeling appreciative to his mom who always negotiated the boys' tensions. Appreciation or gratefulness is a key strategy to reduce anger.

Coffee Klatch The phrase is borrowed from German 'kaffeeklatsch,' translated as *kaffee* = coffee and *klatsch* = gossip. How then do you think we may use this word in English? It simply means a casual social gathering for coffee and conversation. Coffee shops have become very popular for such casual social gathering and conversations. Name a coffee shop in your area.

Boarding and Breaking Horses Boarding

horses – to provide shelter (as in a horse stable) in which horses live; breaking horses – repeated training to accustom a wild (or never-before-ridden) horse to tolerate and finally to accept being led, wearing a saddle, and carrying a rider.

Impertinence means lack of respect; rudeness. How

was Mr. Harold being rude to Mom? Disrespect is a big problem nowadays. Can you name a disrespectful thing that children may say or do? How about adults?

Battle-Broken refers to being broken or scarred or

hurt in a battle. Of course, Arley and his brother were not in a battle, but their adventure became a battle for survival and safety. Afterwards, they were scared and scarred, dirty and worn.

Miscreants Say *mis-kre-ents*. People who misbehave very

badly or actually break laws. Find at least five synonyms for "miscreant" and write them down.

Sentiment is a view, opinion, or attitude toward a

situation that is informed by a strong feeling or emotion.

Beating a Dead Horse Arley already described

this expression or idiom quite well. Another way to explain this idiom: if we continue a particular endeavor when the outcome is already decided, we waste time and energy and sometimes, relationships. It also might be an ongoing argument in the family that never changes. When one is said to be beating a dead horse, he or she never produces any helpful new information, but rather just repeats (beating) the same old ideas.

Another idiom that some people in these situations finally come to express is, "let's agree to disagree." Can you explain this expression?

Conundrum is a difficult question, quandary, dilemma; a puzzle or riddle.

Cavalier Say *kav-a-lir*. Pronounce the "v" clearly and offer the slightest rest before finishing the word. It should almost sound like three syllables rather than two. As a noun, this word has an historical meaning from the time of King Charles I of England, and another definition is a breed of dog. You can search those, if you wish. The definition that fits this context is an adjective meaning an offhanded comment or showing a lack of proper concern. It may also mean too casual or dismissive.

Do you think Chad understood that the police chief did not appreciate his joke?

Bereavement Dinner It is customary, after a funeral service, for a church or other social/civic group to provide a home-cooked dinner for the bereaved, that is, for the family and friends of the deceased or others who attended the funeral.

Dementia a group of symptoms caused by damage or death of nerves in the brain. The symptoms might be loss of memory or language or motor skills. The condition is often associated with aging of the brain causing afflicted elders to talk loudly, repeat sentences, lose short-term memory, engage in unclear (rambling) conversation, and even suffer with hearing impairment, speaking and walking difficulties, etc.

Lucid means easily understood, expressed clearly as opposed to rambling thoughts, overlapping sentences, nonsensical conversations.

Insinuated is to hint indirectly at something unpleasant or bad. Did the relatives give actual accounts of the bad behavior of Mr. Jonathan Harold's and "Grandma Beverly's" dad?

Imploding means to collapse violently inward rather than "explode," which is to blow-up outwardly. The old dirt walls of the child-built tunnels were found to be shifting with various modern vibrations and, in the Ketring family case, their basement tunnel imploded; i.e., first, there was a tunnel the boys found and then it was covered by shifted/fallen dirt; another vibration and it opened again.

Whodunit is a term that stands for "who has done it?" or "who did it?" It refers to a mystery or detective story in which the reader is given clues so they might guess who was the perpetrator before being revealed at the climax of the story. Whodunits often include humor provided by an eccentric or amateur detective (or in this case, a young and newly assigned detective) who proceeds with the investigation.

Research the term "whodunit" to find when the word was coined, the history of mystery, detective, or crime literature. You may also be interested in the famous titles and authors of stories that are considered "whodunits."

Why is this story a mystery? Can you retell the climax of the story by answering, "Whodunit?"

Is there something left unfinished in this story?

Convened means to come together for a meeting or specific activity; summoned; call to order.

Places a Sundry are various, miscellaneous, assorted, several different places.

Ground-Penetrating Radar Machine is a lawn mower-type machine that pulses radar (radio frequency waves) into the ground, seeking a reply of the waves hitting underground voids or obstacles and reading, through a computer type attachment, where the underground map changes.

This topic can be reviewed further by searching the following topics:

- How to find underground caves and tunnels
- Ground penetrating radar
- Seismic activities for finding tunnels
- Military activity – searching for tunnels at border crossings

The last couple of paragraphs of the second section offer an incident of **foreshadowing**. Define the word "foreshadowing" and describe this instance.

Find any **allusions to "light"** in this story, either a natural light, a mechanical light, light of understanding, etc. What is the most interesting "light" in this story to you?

Guide to Parents and Educators

Children experience light and darkness as seen, felt, and awareness—similarly to and perhaps more acutely than adults.

Every good story leaves a footprint of light-dark awareness. This anthology attempts to esteem light—a varied concept, certainly:

- a glittering pond with singing shale
- a sun-kissed wild rabbit leads saviors to her nest
- a blinding snowstorm blows a boy toward manhood
- a hot barren sun oversees the extranormal meeting of cheetah and child
- a mysterious dangling light bulb in an underground tunnel

Children who read these stories well will naturally explore their own reactions to light expressions, to characters, settings, etc. Guide their discoveries by assigning themed word play, poetry, art. Journals and essays often help readers discover their own associative experiences. Spiritual leaders may wish to guide conversations per familial values or religious teachings, especially discussing light and darkness. Exploring life, light, learning, and love never thrives in a vacuum of values or morality.

A section of glossary terms and story questions appears at the end of each story. We include suggestions for lesson plans and classroom experiences. Especially, please encourage readers to read aloud, using voices to dramatize action and characters. Reader's Theater and Call-and-Response (Angela Watson's website thecornerstoneforteachers.com) are two unique ways to marry reading with movement to secure student attention and recall.

Enjoy!
—B. A. Hughes

Story Summaries, Objectives, & Lessons

Spots in the Wind

This story presents a fantasy viewpoint of animals in the wild, assigning proud and lonely feelings, curiosity/desire to interact with humans, and recognizing an extra-sensory connection many people experience with their animals.

From a mini-study about cheetah conservation and African geography to mention of a Biblical story, a phrase from which we use often in modern language, and even a nod to a real-world international society of zoology, story-readers may be guided along a number of auxiliary studies: geography, science, husbandry, conservation.

Most interesting to some readers will be the opportunity to explore their own interpretation of the relationship between Siel and Julia, comparing and contrasting their own experiences with pets, farm animals, or backyard wildlife.

Tracking Big Cat

In a typical story of the fear and bravado of a boy, Sam

faces the opportunity to become a "knight in shining armor." His grandmother figure is treated with respect, humor, and awe. The winter elements provide the antagonist role.

Students may enjoy comparing Big Cat to their own pets: breed, color, personality, name and history in the family, and a time their own pet got lost or ran away.

Sam loved the rich, dark hot chocolate his grandmother made "from scratch." Allow students to find a recipe of favorite drinks (child-appropriate) and assemble the ingredients to make drinks for classroom taste-testing.

We have included a bit of Americana with the mini-study of Carhartt. Perhaps the readers would search for Carhartt pictures or draw themselves in their own winter gear.

Encourage readers to engage their families in this story by creating a rope path in their own yards. Then, they should describe the path in words so that a blind-folded friend could follow it. Math may be explored by assigning distances to each "landmark" and creating story problems.

Middle students should be able to answer what happened at the very end of the story and explore how bits and pieces of daily activities can end up in dreams.

Small Brown

Katja, the protagonist, faces a challenge that pits reason against responsibility in a sort of "coming-of-age" story. Her family members belong to a homeschooling cooperative. In the glossary we offer a mini-study of Home School in the United States. This may suggest an opportunity for readers to compare and contrast public, private, and home/community schooling experiences. The story also provides a short scene to model a successful "family meeting."

A couple of idioms or maxims from this story suggest readers explore creative uses of our language. Perhaps they will create a saying or proverb of their own. Religious leaders may wish to investigate with students the Biblical books of Proverbs and Psalms (and many others) which provide extensive maxims, word play, poetry, and other literary devices (see *Puns and Word Play in the Bible*, by Kent West on YouTube).

This story is pivotal in suggesting, as does the Glimm poem at the beginning of the anthology, that there is more knowledge (light) in the universe, in nature, than what can be explained by science.

Children, as do all people, have a special reaction to their own name. The unusual names in the story may suggest an exploration of the genesis and meaning of students' own names. Especially, they often enjoy asking family members how they got their name.

Transform and Roll Out

Transformer Toys provide a theme of fun and serious play for Bart's family who are separated (for a time) by serious illness. An uncle becomes Bart's mentor and his little twin sisters require him to learn to care for and nurture them. In addition, Bart must shoulder an adult role on the homestead. We see the frustration and eventual breakdown of a boy coming of age.

A mini-study of Transformer Toys allows students to discuss their own toys or collectibles and if/how these are a family collaboration.

For astute and interested students, Transformer Toys may be studied with pre-engineering inquiry regarding the complex moving parts of the toys.

Another study in the glossary highlights the history of and modern notes on Homesteading. This could provide a large classroom study with oral reports, building models, etc.

Slippery Rock

A girl with poor manners and a hurting heart headlines this story—a bit of magic and "old country earthlore" leads Anders to some healing. Readers will enjoy picking up on Anders' rude behaviors and eager to point them out. This is a most teachable moment to discuss manners and respect.

Children may recognize the difficulties of living with one very busy parent, the confusion surrounding the missing parent, and even the relative isolation of living in a high-rise building, often with a low sense of community. This may present prime time to discuss networking, clubs, sports, and church.

One interesting research project might be to allow students to interview older relatives to discover their own heritage: from what part of the world comes your family name? What are some beliefs about nature, superstitions, etc. from experiences and memories of your elders? (Search *StoryCorps*, a national project to instruct and inspire people to record each others' stories, at storycorps.org.)

Finally, the glossary provides a mini geology study which may urge readers to compare ("crying and singing") shale with other rocks with which they may be more familiar.

Underground

This mystery involves two brothers and a neighborhood funeral home. They face a frightening scene inside a tunnel and further fears trying to solve the mystery.

The boys' mother is ill and employs a service dog, Sasha. We offer a question list in the glossary for readers to explore service animals.

Several idioms and foreshadowing are highlighted for language studies.

Math might be invoked to decide distances/diameters of the tunnel(s) or sizes of typical residential lots with the juxtaposition of the family home and the funeral home. Perhaps the whole idea of underground activity might lead to a search of ground-penetrating radar (GPR) machines, mentioned at the end of the story.

In emergency situations the family's pastor provides shelter for the family. Discuss how church and/or community have served others in distressful situations.

In addition, readers may imagine alternative endings or other explanations for the story's mysteries.

Finally, Parents and Educators, please share your own ideas of enhancing these stories for Middle School Readers on the Glimpse Books Facebook page.

Acknowledgments

I deeply appreciate all the people who wish me well in my writing venture. I need cheerleaders more than most.

Don Hart offered me long talks and many of his own stories, which convinced me I should be published. Thank you, Captain!

Jeremy and Heidi Woodall, besides homeschooling our illustrator, took on so many extra responsibilities in moving the publishing process forward, from one side of the country to the other! How I love you!

Kelli Holdeman believes in me more than I have believed in myself. Everyone should have a friend like this. Her interest in reading my work is unflagging. God's blessing on you, CC.

It is hard to not be biased about my illustrator. At just 12 years old, my granddaughter Quinci Woodall managed the six-month project of sketching and re-drawing the illustrations in this book. She took professional criticism in stride, worked under a deadline, and said she loved working for her "Mimi." Kudos, darling!

Biographies

〜〜〜

Photo credit: Kelli Holdeman

B. A. HUGHES writes…in cursive! Pen on notebook paper every day produces the beginnings of youth fiction, poetry, curricula, and journals…thousands of journal entries! In Hughes' library, collected for over five decades, her cursive meanderings fill personal journals and writing journals. There is even a large Mason jar which cradles several dozen quotes and quips on torn colored paper bits.

Glimm, A Glimpse of Light Found is Hughes' first book. A few of her other works have been published in local periodicals. Some of her writing is used as classroom curricula. Hughes was employed as a family advocate for a county government human services organization in the Midwest. Later, she directed marketing for a hospice agency. Perhaps more importantly, Hughes rode her bicycle 60 miles on her 60th birthday without training…just because.

Hughes' happiest and hardest life project was rearing her own six children and now, loving her 13 grans! She writes from her home in the Midwest United States with one jealous tabby cat on her lap.

Photo credit: Jeremy and Heidi Woodall

QUINCI M. WOODALL, the book's illustrator, was born in Ohio in 2004 and later grew up in Fort Wayne, Indiana. Crossing the country, she currently lives near Salem, Oregon, with her parents, and her brother, Copeland. Ever since Quinci could hold a pencil she has loved drawing, drawing all the time! She has been crowned resident artist in her school classroom five years running. Recently, Quinci has become an award-winning artist for pencil drawing in her art school. When not drawing, Quinci reads, typically about animals, which is her other love. Having cared for many animals, her present favorite is her lop-eared rabbit, Nutmeg. As an experienced rabbit owner, Quinci is now embarking on breeding. With a strong intent to pursue animal husbandry as a career, Quinci plans to creatively blend her love for drawing and animals in her life's career. Therefore, she enthusiastically jumped at the opportunity to illustrate stories for B. A. Hughes, her beloved grandma, "Mimi."

Made in the USA
Columbia, SC
01 October 2017